EYE CANDY

Read all the books in the

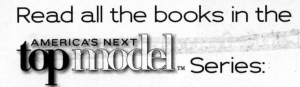 Series:

1: Face Value

2: Eye Candy

EYE CANDY

Taryn Bell

Scholastic Inc.
New York Toronto London Auckland
Sydney Mexico City New Delhi Hong Kong

Published by Scholastic Inc. SCHOLASTIC and associated logos are trademarks and/or registered trademarks of Scholastic Inc.

ISBN-13: 978-0-545-14112-3
ISBN-10: 0-545-14112-5

12 11 10 9 8 7 6 5 4 3 2 1   9 10 11 12 13 14/0

Printed in the U.S.A.
First edition, August 2009

TOP MODEL
PREPARATORY
SUMMER PROGRAM
A DIVISION OF
AMERICA'S NEXT TOP
MODEL AGENCY, INC.

235 Spring Street
New York, NY 10012

Dear Students:

Happy July!

It has recently come to my attention that several of you have gotten a bit, shall we say, relaxed in regards to our program's rules. May I remind you that we at Top Model Prep pride ourselves on our honesty, integrity, and the positive image we promote. Founded on the wild success of the hit television show, *America's Next Top Model*, our high-end agency, and this ultraprestigious summer program, represent the very best the modeling world has to offer. And you ladies, in turn, represent *us*.

As you all know, this is a two-month program with competitions—and eliminations—held every two weeks. The remaining model-student with the highest score at summer's end will receive top prize and top honors. However, winning is not just about walking well and looking gorgeous on camera. It's also about playing by the rules. In this case, that means keeping to your curfew, signing in and out of the Top Model Apartments in SoHo, and attending classes on time.

And there other ways to be eliminated from the program than by losing a challenge, if I make myself crystal clear.

I trust I will not have to write you about this matter again.

Yours in beauty,

Victoria Devachan
Headmistress

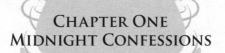

CHAPTER ONE
MIDNIGHT CONFESSIONS

It had been, without a doubt, the worst night in all of Alexis Cournos's sixteen years.

"I cannot *believe* we were almost arrested!" growled her roommate and competitor Lindsay Robinson, marching into the common room of apartment 14C. Alexis, already huddled into an armchair, her long auburn ringlets shielding her face, watched as Lindsay kicked off her high-heeled booties. For the hundredth time that night, Alexis bit back her tears.

"Well, we weren't," their other roommate and fellow model-hopeful, Shiva-Rose Safir, told Lindsay in her pragmatic way as she slipped out of her cropped blazer. She opened the window, letting in the sultry summer breeze of a late, late New York City night. Outside, taxicabs honked their horns and a siren wailed.

A police siren, Alexis thought, shivering.

"It was still a nightmare, being hauled away from our table like that," moaned the fourth roommate — and everyone's biggest competitor — Chloe Huntley. She collapsed on the sofa, running a hand through her corn-silk blond hair and easing her feet out of her satin peep-toe pumps. "Thank God there weren't any paparazzi around to get pictures. Can you imagine?"

"What do you care?" Lindsay asked Chloe, narrowing her eyes. "I thought you were dropping out of the program, leaving NYC." Chloe had dropped that bombshell right before Alexis's own personal bomb had gone off.

"Whatever," Chloe sniffed, plucking her ever-present iPhone from her clutch and avoiding Lindsay's question.

Alexis bit her glossy bottom lip as all her roommates finally turned and glared at her. There was a moment of stony silence. Then Lindsay seemed to speak for the rest of them when she snapped: "What on earth were you *thinking*?"

Alexis hugged herself, wishing she could disappear. Being a part of this program meant so much to her — and now she had to go and mess it all up, right after winning the first competition!

"I'm sorry," she said in a hoarse whisper, feeling her eyes well with hot tears. "I had no idea this would happen."

In disbelief, Lindsay shook out her dark curls. "Oh, so you're saying that when you went to Max Brenner the first time and stole stuff, and then when you went back a second time and stole stuff again, it never occurred to you, never crossed your mind that maybe, just maybe you might possibly, oh, I don't know, get *caught*?" Lindsay put her hands on her hips, her gold bangles clinking together. "And then you perform the ultimate act of genius and go back a third time! What, were you absent the day they taught the whole 'never return to the scene of the crime' lesson in shoplifter's school?"

"I never got caught before," grumbled Alexis — then immediately regretted her words.

"Wait a minute," said Shiva-Rose, striding over to stand beside Lindsay. Her olive complexion was now flushed with pink. "You mean you've done this before? I totally knew it."

Alexis squirmed in her seat but didn't comment. "I'm sorry," she said again.

"So let's recap," said Chloe from her perch on the couch, twirling her long pearl necklace around her finger. "When the four of us went to Max Brenner at the start of the summer, you snuck off, saying you had to use the restroom, but in reality you went to the gift shop and swiped a bunch of stupid collectibles and chocolate. And you got away with it."

"She *thought* she got away with it," clarified Lindsay.

Chloe ignored the interruption. "And then, you went back to the same restaurant on a date with what's-his-name. . . ."

"Shane," said Alexis, feeling herself blush at the thought of her charming, adorable male-model crush. What would he think of her *now*?

"And you stole some more stuff. And once again you thought you were in the clear."

"But when we went back there again tonight," said Shiva-Rose, picking up where Chloe left off, "you were recognized because even though you made it out of the place with your loot the first time—"

"The first *two* times," interjected Lindsay in a scathing tone.

"You had, in fact, been caught on the security cameras," Shiva-Rose finished, her Israeli accent made even thicker by her gathering anger. Alexis had come to consider Shiva-Rose, out of the other three girls, something of a friend. It was painful to now see her so miffed.

Chloe gasped as something occurred to her. "What if you'd been wearing your Top Model Prep T-shirt! You would have started a *huge* scandal for the program."

"Well, I wasn't," Alexis snapped, sitting up straighter. She no longer felt like crying; she was moving from distraught to slightly annoyed. Yes, she'd made a giant mistake, but couldn't her roommates be an inch more supportive?

"Hey, don't you get snarky with us," said Lindsay. "You put us all in a horrible position tonight. Do you think any of us can ever go back to that restaurant again? And if any of this got back to Victoria, you'd be on the first bus back to wherever you come from. Not that I'd care."

Shiva-Rose nodded. "The only reason they let us walk out of the restaurant is because Chloe paid for all your stuff on her credit card, *and* promised to have her mother make an appearance at the place."

Alexis thought back to the awful scene in the back room at Max Brenner, where she'd broken down in front of the manager and her roommates. Thankfully, Chloe had kept a cool head and assured the manager (who, like most men in America, would give his right arm to meet the gorgeous Charlotte Huntley) that her famous model mom would not only show up but pose for pictures and endorse the establishment in print, just to keep him from pressing charges against Alexis. It had taken a lot of wheedling and flashing of Chloe's black AmEx card, but the manager had finally relented.

"What I don't get," said Lindsay, finally sitting down — as far as possible from Chloe — on the sofa, "is why you'd steal a bunch of junk from a chocolate-themed restaurant's gift shop."

"What I don't get," added Chloe in an icy tone, "is why you'd steal at all."

Easy for you to say, Alexis thought. *You grew up in a mansion in Beverly Hills. You've always had everything you ever wanted*. But she couldn't say that. Especially not since Chloe had saved her butt.

"Still," said Lindsay, "moral platitudes aside, if you're going to take stuff, why don't you go somewhere worthy, like the Prada boutique or the Apple Store?"

Been there, stole that, thought Alexis, but again, she kept her mouth shut.

Shiva-Rose's long-lashed dark eyes went wide as a realization seemed to sweep over her. "The first time we went to Max Brenner you paid with a credit card. Don't tell me . . ."

Alexis lowered her gaze, her cheeks warm. "Yeah. I took it off one of the nearby tables and forged the signature."

"You stole some random person's credit card?" cried Chloe.

"Yes, but I swear, I made only that one charge, and I destroyed the card the minute we got home," Alexis said, hoping the interrogation would end soon. All she wanted to do was wash her tearstained face and go to sleep.

And dream this had never happened.

"Well, at least you used your head *then*," said Lindsay, shaking her head. "You definitely would have gotten caught if you started charging things. This one time, my friend, Juliet Rivers, had her platinum card stolen and some sleazeball started charging thousands of dollars worth of junk. After she reported the card stolen they caught him."

Chloe blinked her blue eyes, then glanced sharply at Lindsay. "*You're* friends with Juliet Rivers?" she asked, sounding astonished that Lindsay would be associated with the hot young actress.

"As a matter of fact, I am," Lindsay retorted, glowering at Chloe.

"They were on the TV show together," Shiva-Rose explained, easing down onto the couch's arm and tapping one platform-shod foot. "Remember? She played Lindsay's neighbor, or something."

"Are you guys still in touch?" asked Alexis, glad the subject had changed from her illegal activities to Lindsay's apparent BFF.

"We talk all the time," said Lindsay arrogantly.

"It must be hard," said Shiva-Rose. "Since she's out working in LA and you're . . ." Realizing her mistake, Shiva-Rose trailed off, biting her lip and looking away.

Exiled in New York City, Alexis thought, finishing Shiva-Rose's sentence.

Lindsay didn't reply, but she set her jaw. Alexis knew Lindsay hated that long after the cancellation of her TV series, *Yes, We Blend*, Juliet continued to get TV and film work and Lindsay didn't. Which was why she'd enrolled in Top Model Prep in the first place. She'd made it clear that this program was going to be her ticket back to stardom.

But what will this program mean for me? Alexis wondered, her stomach tightening. Before the disaster at Max Brenner, after all, she'd been riding high—the first winner of the first challenge! Flushed from her victory, she'd even gone ahead and allowed herself to think that, at summer's end, she might very well win the whole thing. Yes, her—ordinary, freckled, under-the-standard-modeling-height Alexis from small-town Michigan. The one who wasn't exotic and international like Shiva-Rose, who wasn't a former child star and a Beyoncé clone like Lindsay, or the one who wasn't a modeling heiress and a natural beauty like Chloe.

She, because of her wits and her talent, still had every chance to come out on top.

Nothing could bring her down.

Except for her very own self.

Alexis sighed as she finally rose from the chair.

"Hey, Alexis?" said Shiva-Rose, her tone suggesting that she wasn't going to get away so easily. "Just make us a promise, okay? That you won't ever shoplift again?"

"I promise," Alexis said, meeting Shiva-Rose's stern gaze, then looking at Lindsay's suspicious expression, and then nodding at Chloe, who now seemed distracted. Eager to escape her roommates at last, Alexis headed for the bathroom.

She knew the other girls had every right to be furious at her, had every right to make demands of her. She could have been thrown in jail. Kicked out of the program. Shipped back home. She'd narrowly escaped the long arm of the law tonight, and knew she might not be so lucky again.

So there was only one thing for Alexis to do from now on.

She had to be more careful.

CHAPTER TWO
CHANGE OF PLANS

Chloe usually took her time pampering herself before bed: There was her five-minute-long tooth-brushing-and-flossing routine (it wasn't easy keeping her veneers so gleaming white), and her careful application of Bliss Cleansing Milk, followed by La Mer face cream. If there was anything her mother had taught her, it was that looking beautiful took effort.

Tonight, though, after Alexis and the others had finally gone to bed in their shared triple, Chloe rushed through her washing-up. With her face still damp, she hurried into her coveted single room, locked the door, and flung herself on the bed. Then, her heart pounding, she whipped out her iPhone.

She couldn't believe it!

Lindsay hadn't realized it at all, but earlier, in the common room, the former celeb turned wannabe model had revealed an amazingly important detail. A clue.

Chloe's boyfriend back home, Liam Lattimore, had been seen gallivanting around LA with none other than Juliet Rivers. That was why Chloe had wanted to leave the program. Liam was the love of her life, and he meant much more to her than a career in modeling. She had to try and salvage their relationship. But now Chloe understood. The coincidence was too much. Liam was being seen with Juliet because he'd been set up. Chloe knew what a scheming mastermind Lindsay was. Now she'd gone too far.

Fuming, Chloe tapped out a text message to Liam:

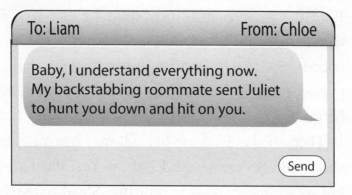

To: Liam   From: Chloe

Baby, I understand everything now. My backstabbing roommate sent Juliet to hunt you down and hit on you.

Send

She imagined her words bouncing from one cell tower to another as they crossed the country.

Awaiting his response, she practically held her breath. His reply came quickly, which she figured was a good thing — it meant his hands were free to type a message, as opposed to being all over Juliet Rivers. The text said:

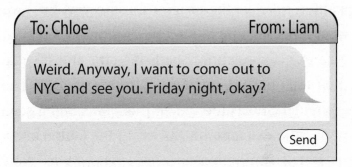

To: Chloe   From: Liam

Weird. Anyway, I want to come out to NYC and see you. Friday night, okay?

Send

Weird? She'd been hoping for an adamant denial of any interest whatsoever in Juliet Rivers, but for now this response was enough. If Liam thought this Juliet witch was playing him just as a favor to Lindsay, his pride would keep him from spending any more time with her.

She sent him a reply text that said Friday would be perfect.

Then she lay back on her pillows, vowing that she would get even with Lindsay. Yes, she'd told her roommates she was quitting. She'd planned to leave Top Model Prep behind. But suddenly, Chloe Huntley had a change of heart. Her plan to drop out and go home would have to be altered.

Her new plan was to defeat Lindsay. Her new plan was to win!

The next day, at noon sharp, Chloe entered the common room dressed impeccably for their Challenge Two Orientation. After some thought, she'd put on a strapless pale pink Alexander McQueen sundress, flawless makeup, and wedge espadrilles. Shiva-Rose, downing a cup of coffee, wore a white tank that showed off her broad shoulders and a flowy white skirt. The effect was a little bit too hippie-chick for New York, Chloe decided. Alexis, still looking pale and haggard—she probably hadn't slept at all—wore a purple tee tucked into short-shorts and floral-print heels. Definitely more fashionable than the jeans and flip-flops the red-haired girl had sported throughout the first session. And Lindsay, who was checking her watch obsessively, wore a yellow halter dress and matching flats. Her simple, chic outfit came the closest to Chloe's in terms of fabulosity, but Chloe noted with triumph that not one of her roommates looked as put together as she did.

An expression that was half fury, half panic registered on Lindsay's face. "Tell me that's the outfit you're wearing on the plane," she said. "Tell me your luggage is already in the hall. . . ."

"Give it up, Lindsay," Chloe said, triumphantly tossing her golden locks over one shoulder. "I've decided to stay."

"You have?" Lindsay's eyes flashed.

Chloe could almost read her mind: *After all the work I've done? After all my plotting to turn you into an emotional train wreck, just to force you to go home in desperation and beg your boyfriend to come back to you so I could win?*

"I'm staying," repeated Chloe, then added silently, *And you're goin' down.*

"Let's go, then," said Shiva-Rose. "The car is waiting downstairs."

The car turned out to be what was called a "party bus." The thirty remaining girls who'd survived the first challenge were being driven to a surprise location where they would have breakfast and learn what was in store for them over the next two weeks.

Most of the girls had never experienced this mode of transportation before and were thrilled by the interior of the vehicle designed specifically to transport "party people" from one place to another while providing optimal enjoyment. It featured a ginormous U-shaped couch, stocked minibars, flat-screen TVs, and—not wasted on this group—full-length mirrors. The stereo system rivaled that of many dance clubs; over the speakers, Jesse McCartney was asking, "How do you sleep?" Many of the girls—even a more pert-looking Alexis—danced in the seats to the infectious beat as the bus zoomed through the busy streets.

Chloe was oblivious. She'd been in such deluxe rides before. Besides, she had more pressing matters on her mind. She'd spent half the night cleaning up the mess Lindsay had attempted to create by texting all of her LA friends and explaining the Juliet situation. Liam hadn't cheated on her; he'd been punk'd.

Of course, deep down, Chloe knew that whether Juliet had entered Liam's life on Lindsay's instructions or entirely by accident wasn't really the point. He could have—*should* have—ignored her come-ons. Chloe knew this, but she was going to try to overlook it. She liked to think that under similar circumstances she would easily resist temptation. Guys hit on her all the time and her response was always the same: *I'm flattered, but I have a boyfriend.* She had yet to meet a boy that caused her to doubt her feelings for Liam.

Chloe's iPhone rang. She answered it without even looking at the screen, thinking it would be Sara, responding to the news of Liam's innocence.

"Chloe?"

It was her mother.

Chloe's stomach sank.

"Hi, Mom." Chloe pressed the phone tight to one ear and covered the other with her hand so she could hear over the music and squeals. "What's up?"

"Why did I have to hear from Victoria, and not you, that you lost the first challenge?" her mother demanded. "More important, why did you lose?"

"It was a rock-and-roll thing," Chloe explained. "I don't really have the rock-and-roll look. Plus, there was a chemistry issue." She dropped her voice to a whisper, even though she didn't care if Lindsay heard her. "The girl I was photographed with is kind of my mortal enemy."

"I expect more from you, Chloe."

"I know."

In her head, Chloe composed a poem:

Expectations

Demands

The weight of the world

On my shoulders

I want to be weightless

I want to be free

She wished she could type the poem out and send it to Liam. He was the only one who understood that she had a poet's soul. That her heart was not in the runway or in photo shoots but in words and language. She wished her mother would get that, at least a little bit.

The song on the stereo faded into another, older Jesse McCartney release.

"Do I hear a boy's voice in the background?" demanded Charlotte.

"Yes, Mom. It's Jesse McCartney."

"Oh, good. He's cute. And famous. Make sure someone sees you together. Try to get pictures."

"He's not here, Mom. It's on the radio."

"Oh. Well, we should arrange for you to meet him. For a photo op. I'll call his agent."

Jesse, in his sweet, alluring voice, was singing: "Don't stress, don't stress, don't stress, girl . . ."

Chloe decided to heed his advice.

"I have to go, Mom," she said curtly.

And before Charlotte could launch into a full-fledged lecture on the importance of Chloe following in her Manolo Blahnik–wearing footsteps, Chloe hung up.

Chapter Three
A Challenge Revealed

Top Model Prep Summer Schedule

- Session Two: July 16 – July 31
- Competitors: 30
- Challenge: Will be revealed today!
- Date of challenge: July 31
- Scoring: In the competition, individual grades ranging from A+ to D- will be given out by our expert panel.
- Eliminations: Ten girls with the lowest combined scores will be asked to leave the program immediately.
- Winner: The girl with the highest score for this challenge will be named the winner of Session Two.

Lindsay was still fuming over Chloe's decision to stay — had *all* her careful planning and texting and maneuvering gone wrong somehow? — when the bus pulled into Manhattan's trendy Meatpacking

District. Here, the cobblestone streets teemed with fashionistas and the most up-and-coming restaurants and shops. Their swank ride stopped in front of one such elegant restaurant, called Del Posto. Lindsay knew from her extensive blog-and-magazine reading that it was currently one of the hottest spots in town. She could see why.

The girls oohed and ahhed as they made their way inside, pointing out the polished marble floors and rich dark wood paneling. The center-piece of Del Posto was a wide, elegant staircase that led to a balcony reserved for guests of the highest caliber. Seated in the balcony, these VIPs could literally (and figuratively) look down on the people in the lounge or bar area.

Apparently, Top Model Prep was going all out because today the balcony was reserved for the models. The blond hostess led them up the gorgeous stairs like an angel leading them to heaven.

This is so *how I roll*, thought Lindsay. *Or how I should roll anyway.* Since her series had been canceled, she hadn't been rolling much at all. In fact she'd pretty much come to a complete halt, as though her tires had been slashed. But all that was going to change. Chloe's decision to stay notwithstanding, Lindsay still had every intention of winning this thing and getting back on the A-list.

Lindsay scanned the upstairs seating area, noticing the place settings at the round tables. The 14C roommates were sharing a table with Jana, Ava, and Faye—the remaining girls who roomed across the hall in 14A.

"This is so amazing," said Faye, her black eyes shining as the girls took their seats. Instantly, a phalanx of synchronized waitstaff descended upon them, pouring sparkling water into their delicate-stemmed glasses.

Then, without explanation, another group of waiters materialized and set two-foot-high cushioned wicker footstools on the floor next to each girl.

"We get to put our feet up!" exclaimed Jana, who proceeded to do just that.

"For real?" said Ava doubtfully.

"I don't think you're supposed to put your feet up," Shiva-Rose leaned in and whispered. "It's for something else."

"What?" Lindsay chuckled. "Your Chihuahua?"

With an exasperated sigh, Chloe lazily slipped her Burberry bag off her shoulder and onto the footstool.

Lindsay bristled at the fact that Chloe knew something that Lindsay didn't. This was the kind of esoteric knowledge that only people of Chloe's circle would know. These footstool-type objects were perches for pricey handbags. Made sense, too. No luxury tote or diamond-encrusted clutch should ever have to suffer the indignity of coming into contact with the floor. Lindsay vowed that after she won, she would demand a handbag holder every time she set foot in a restaurant. Even if it was McDonald's. *"Gimme a Big Mac and fries, and don't forget the purse holder."*

Just then, Victoria Devachan, their headmistress and former fashion-force-to-be-reckoned-with, stood up in front of the group. She was wearing a white silk jumpsuit, which caused a few whispers. Were jumpsuits back in style? Lindsay was pretty sure that if Victoria was sporting one, they were definitely high on the must-have list. Again. Jumpsuits are like cockroaches, Lindsay decided. They never die. Every decade or so they make a brief comeback, during which all the current fashion gurus gush over how sporty and stylish they are, how you can dress them up or down, yadda yadda yadda, all the while pretending that just a few years ago they hadn't turned up their noses and scoffed, "Remember jumpsuits? What were we thinking?"

Regardless, Victoria was presently in favor of the jumpsuit, and she looked stunning. Her pale skin was baby-smooth, her eyes showed no signs of drooping, her carrot-colored hair, loosely curly, tickled her chin. Combined with her stick-straight posture and supreme poise, Victoria knew what it meant to "represent." She was exactly what a former "It Girl" and current CEO of a thriving business should look like.

"I want to welcome you to our second session," Victoria announced. "Congratulations on making it this far. I'm so proud. I think this year's models are the best in all our history!"

True or not, the compliment was met with a burst of self-congratulatory applause. Lindsay snuck a glance at Alexis, who was looking guilty and pale. *Will she crack?* Lindsay wondered. Then she peeked at Chloe, whose chin was raised and whose expression was fiercely determined. Lindsay longed for the meek, weepy Chloe of yesterday. *Sigh*. Shiva-Rose, just as she had during the first orientation, whipped out a pen and pad and was taking *notes*. Girl couldn't help herself from being a good student. So annoying.

"I hope you're enjoying being at Del Posto," Victoria went on, beaming. "For those of you who don't know, this restaurant is the domain of the magnificently talented chef Mario Batali, and he has instructed his sous-chefs to prepare all of his very best dishes for you." On cue, the team of waiters reappeared, bearing trays laden with delicious-looking pastas and salads. "So . . . no nibbling. You're not bunnies, you're models! And there *is* a difference."

Against her will, Lindsay remembered something Chloe had said last week, about the model's mantra: *Grow a thick skin, remain stick thin.*

Lindsay had endured a public battle with her own weight and knew that for many of the girls, food was the enemy. But Victoria clearly believed that there was nothing more beautiful than a healthy body. At Top Model Prep, the girls were advised to continue to eat well, to balance their diet, and not to be afraid to indulge themselves when the opportunity arose. Exercise was good, obsession was bad. TMP's mantra was "role model before fashion model."

Theoretically, it was a noble stance. Realistically, Lindsay knew, it was impossible. In the real world, these girls would have to claw their way to the top in designer clothes and stiletto heels. In Lindsay's experience, designers designed for nothing wider than a wire hanger. Maybe that would change someday. Someday was not this day. At the end of the summer, intentional or not, a thinner-than-average girl would win. *Bet on it.*

"We've invited you here to expose you to the world's finest cuisine, to describe your new classes, and of course — what you're really all waiting for — to reveal our second challenge! But first, please say hello to the teachers, coaches, and panel members who've helped you get this far."

First up was creative director Dan'yel Fieldstone, who rose from his seat and blew a kiss to the girls. Lindsay liked Dan'yel. Smart and simpatico, he truly had their best interests at heart. It was Dan'yel who provided a shoulder for weepy models to cry on, Dan'yel whose wry sense of humor was just so New York you felt included every time, Dan'yel whose advice they took most seriously; and even though he could be direct in his criticism, he was never hurtful.

Next up was Mack Scarborough (*phony-name alert!* thought Lindsay), who stood lazily and winked at his audience. Top Model's house photographer took amazing photos and was himself savagely beautiful, slim, and scruffy, today rocking a pair of 7 For All Mankind jeans and a denim shirt, calculated to bring out his eyes to max effect. Today — as they'd been every day since the start of the program — Mack's sights were set on one female in particular: Shiva-Rose Safir. Something had transpired between the two. Lindsay didn't know what exactly, but she'd find out and use it against Shiva-Rose, if necessary.

Then came stylist Anabelle Trembley, who clasped her hands together as if in prayer and bowed to the girls. Anabelle was a theatrical, certifiable loon who believed in inner beauty, holistic balance, and Gwyneth Paltrow's Web site, GOOP. A self-appointed caretaker of their spiritual lives, pretty much whatever wisdom Anabelle imparted made Lindsay want to gag.

The fourth person on the panel was La Aura B. Lindsay despised the in-house designer. La Aura B was a mousy mess with a mean streak whose "fashions" looked as if they'd been through a paper shredder.

This freaky foursome held her future in their hands.

Lindsay gulped down her sparkling water and lifted her fork. The pasta smelled amazing.

Then she paused, realizing there was a fifth, conspicuously empty seat at Victoria's table.

"Now I will tell you about this session's classes," said Victoria, snapping open her white laptop. Through the magic of PowerPoint, a giant screen lit up behind her.

During the first session, they'd taken classes in runway walking, photo shoot interpretation, and makeup application. This pretty much covered the spectrum of skills they'd need.

"I hope we get to do more makeup lessons," Shiva-Rose whispered, popping an olive into her mouth.

"We've gotta get more fashion this time," said Jana, spearing a cherry tomato. "I'm all about clothes."

"They should do accessories, like how to put outfits together. I could use some help in that area," Faye said.

But the list that appeared on the screen showed none of those things. Lindsay's heart sped up. If she was right about what these classes portended, this was going to be an amazing session.

Second Session Classes

- Acting Technique — Basics
- Body Language & Expression
- Script Reading
- Elocution
- Memorization and Teleprompters
- Fashion Choices

"As you can see," Victoria pointed out with a sly smile, "these classes are very different from last semester's curriculum. You might even wonder what they have to do with modeling. But as you'll learn, there are many different modeling opportunities, and our job is to prepare you for all of them."

"What's electrocution got to do with it?" Ava asked, her wide eyes scrolling down the class list. "Is that like waxing?"

"It's el-o-*cu*-tion," Faye schooled her. "It means pronouncing things correctly. Using proper diction."

"For what?" asked clueless Jana.

Lindsay couldn't help but roll her eyes. At least her roommates, aggravating as they were, had some amount of brains.

She stole a glance at Alexis, who was pushing her food around the plate. In her short time in New York, adorable Alexis had not only stolen a bunch of merchandise but also the heart of a gorgeous male model. The girl was definitely on a lucky streak. She got the guy and she won the first challenge. But Lindsay didn't really see her as a threat. First of all, based on her self-destructive behavior, Alexis would probably implode on her own. If not, she might have a shot at doing catalogue work as a petite model. But it was called "high" fashion for a reason. Anyone under five-nine need not apply.

Shiva-Rose was definitely the right height. She was also smarter than average, and somehow she'd gotten photographer Mack under her spell. But the girl was too moral for her own good; she hadn't taken Mack up on his offer to help her with the last challenge. Plus, her accent and her unfamiliarity with American pop culture (*Yes, We Blend* notwithstanding, of course) put her at a disadvantage.

The real competition at this clambake was Chloe. Lindsay had thought she'd handled her by siccing Juliet Rivers on Chloe's boy toy, Liam. But, Lindsay now realized with a feeling of dread, she'd blown her efforts by revealing her friendship with Juliet last night. Chloe must have put the pieces together. *Why didn't I keep my mouth shut?* Lindsay chided herself. But whatever. Liam was still Chloe's weakness, and Lindsay would just have to try another tack to bring the supermodel-spawn down.

Of course, if she were right about the about-to-be-revealed challenge, Lindsay wouldn't even have to resort to evil tactics at all.

"Are you ready?" asked Victoria as she unveiled the last slide, "Here's your big challenge!"

Big Challenge, Big Win!
- Audition for a national television commercial!
- The highest scorer will automatically be booked for the TV commercial and receive a standard five-figure fee.

The balcony erupted in shrieks, OMGs, gasps, and, in the case of Jana, tears. This was huge, and everyone knew it: a chance to be on TV! And get a huge paycheck! Lindsay had half a mind to go up to Victoria at the podium and accept her prize right now. She was the only one in the room who could win this one. She was an actress!

"The challenge is this: to audition for a national ad campaign for a new line of hair products called Mane Event," Victoria explained. "Once again, your instructors will guide you on your journey to commercial stardom." Now the headmistress effected a heartsick look. "With one exception. Our beloved La Aura B will not be joining us for this challenge."

A murmur of curiosity rippled through the crowd of models. Luckily, Lindsay had just popped a canapé into her mouth; if she hadn't, she might have sprung up from her seat and shouted "Whoo hoo!" at the top of her lungs.

"The reason is an exciting one. La Aura B has been invited to Paris to work alongside Catherine Malandrino. Of course, we here at Top Model Prep wish her nothing but the very best."

The models offered a round of polite applause. Lindsay considered making it a standing ovation. That no-talent ninny was out of here! No more-a La Aura! Could this day get any better?

La Aura stood and made a little speech. It was unclear whether this position overseas was permanent, or only a temporary gig, and the designer would be back for Challenge Three. Lindsay hoped the defection would be forever, but if it wasn't, and La Horror did return for the final showdown, at least Lindsay would be able to get through this latest commercial challenge without wearing any of those hideous clothes!

La Aura B returned to her seat, and Victoria stepped back up to the podium. "Taking La Aura's place on the panel will be a very special guest, the undisputed expert in the field."

She paused dramatically and did a quarter turn to face the top of the staircase. A tall, trim, and immaculately dressed man ascended the stairs and greeted them with a dazzling smile.

For Lindsay, this man needed no introduction. Mario Batali's signature appetizers suddenly curdled in her stomach as she watched this man, her nemesis, approach the podium and shake Victoria's hand.

Victoria gestured to the man. "I'm sure you've all heard of Robert McClary. He's a former actor and now a renowned acting coach whose best-selling book, *Take One*, is the bible for anyone trying to break into show business. His classes are impossible to get into. He's credited with jump-starting the careers of dozens of A-list actors. Everybody wants him, but for the next two weeks, we've got him!"

I already had him, thought Lindsay as she watched her former acting coach take a seat at the head table. *And I hated him.*

CHAPTER FOUR
DRAMA QUEENS

This will not go well, Shiva-Rose thought nervously as she hurried into acting class the next day. She had been dreading the possibility that a TV commercial might be one of the four big challenges, because it was guaranteed to sink her. And here it was. As she took a seat beside her roommates, her fingers automatically went to the pendant she wore around her neck, a heart-shaped locket with a photo of her mother tucked inside.

While she took smoldering photographs and could learn to rock the runway and develop a fashion style, Shiva-Rose had no interest in, or aptitude for, commercials. Actors did TV commercials. Or sometimes, for a specific hair or makeup product, models were featured. But public speaking, and worse, acting, were way outside Shiva-Rose's comfort zone.

"I'm soooo psyched for this!" Ava declared, taking a seat in the row behind Shiva-Rose and the girls from 14C.

"I bet we get a director's chair with our name on it," predicted Jana.

"Getting a TV commercial is so much better than what you won, Alexis — what was it again, some one-page feature in *Seventeen*?" Faye, who'd never been mean before, taunted.

"What makes you think I won't win this one, too?" Alexis whirled around to glower at Faye.

"Yeah," said Lindsay dryly. "She might just *steal* the show."

Shiva-Rose's heart skipped a beat. The roommates had all but sworn an oath of secrecy. As much rivalry as there was in this competition, no one was going to rat Alexis out.

Right?

Alexis turned her scowl to Lindsay. "Funny."

"I would think *you* would be expecting to win this one," Chloe said to Lindsay, pulling a lock of blond hair in front of her eyes and examining it for split ends. "I mean, after all, you are the former child star. Operative word — *former.*"

"Chloe," Shiva-Rose murmured warningly. She was always playing peacekeeper.

"I would, if it were going to be fair," Lindsay sighed, cupping her chin in her hands and looking more vulnerable than Shiva-Rose had ever seen her. "But if Robert McClary is involved in the voting, I might as well just go home now. The man hates me."

"Why?" asked Faye.

"Because he's *met* her," said Chloe.

Alexis hid her giggle behind her hand. Shiva-Rose was relieved to see the girl laugh. Ever since The Incident, her redheaded roommate had been sullen and silent.

"Because," Lindsay clarified, sitting up tall, "when I was six years old, I went to a children's acting workshop. One workshop. He was teaching it. Naturally, I was the best one in the class. But not because of anything he did. He talked about objectives and motivation and finding our centers. We were kindergartners. We had no idea what he was talking about. Anyway, the exercise was to say a few lines about a lost puppy, then cry on cue. None of the other little kids knew how to do it. But I went up there, nailed the dialogue, and then I dropped my face into my hands and sobbed like a champ. When I picked my head up, my face was streaked with tears, and McClary was on the phone to every agent he knew, telling them he had the next big thing right there in his studio."

Lindsay's eyes glowed as she told her tale, and Shiva-Rose understood what pride Lindsay took in her talent. *If only I had an ounce of that acting ability*, Shiva-Rose thought enviously.

"So that's how you got your first agent?" asked Ava. "It sounds as if he loves you!"

"No," said Lindsay. "My mother had already sent my photo out to a bunch of agencies. Just the day before, one of them had called and said they'd like to see me the following morning. It turned out to be one of the agents McClary was calling, but the thing was, I already had the appointment scheduled, so technically, McClary didn't get me the interview. Which meant he wasn't entitled to any kind of kickback when I landed the role on *Yes, We Blend*. So McClary felt as if he'd been tricked. And he's hated me ever since."

The door to the classroom creaked open. McClary entered the room then, and Shiva-Rose eyed him, wondering if Lindsay was just biased. The girl had it in for practically everyone, and McClary seemed fine.

"A few rules," he said, taking a seat behind the desk at the front of the room. "No chatter when I'm speaking. No bathroom breaks. No opting out of class exercises. If you're tardy for class, don't bother coming. I expect professionalism. This is an acting class, ladies. I know you intend to make a living off your looks, but you'll find they will get you only so far. If you're serious about being half good enough to book this commercial, you'll pay attention to everything I say."

Condescending and *narcissistic*, Shiva-Rose thought, suddenly irritated. Was it possible Lindsay was right about him?

He stood and began walking a measured pace around the room as he talked, probably to show off his perfect posture or maybe his Gucci loafers. "In this class, you'll learn how to express yourselves, how to move in front of the camera, how to communicate with an audience."

"How to talk and chew gum at the same time?" Lindsay muttered.

"Ms. Robinson," McClary called her out, "was there something you needed to share with your fellow models?"

Shiva-Rose held her breath. Was Lindsay brave—or stupid—enough to get in his face?

"I was just saying how excited I am to get started," Lindsay said with false sweetness.

"Then let's." He went to the desk again, opened his briefcase, and took out a stack of pages. "If you were auditioning for a real movie or television show, these lines, these snippets of dialogue would be called 'sides.' I want you to take a moment and learn them. Then I'll have you perform them."

McClary began handing out the stack of pages. When Shiva-Rose passed a sheet to Lindsay, she heard her roommate let out a small snort and whisper, "No. Way. Is he *serious*?"

"What is it?" Shiva-Rose whispered, leaning closer.

"I can't believe it," Lindsay whispered back, shaking her head in shock. "These are the same ridiculous lines he gave out in the children's acting workshop ten years ago. Talk about a lack of imagination!"

"Do you think he remembers you?" Shiva-Rose whispered, glancing from the teacher to Lindsay.

Lindsay shrugged. "Well, he's been holding a grudge about that day for the last decade. You'd think he'd recall it with some clarity. But maybe not."

The object of Lindsay's scorn returned to the front of the room.

"I want you to imagine that you have a puppy . . ." McClary began soberly, gazing at each of the girls. "And that your puppy is lost . . ."

Lindsay clearly couldn't help herself. She cracked up laughing.

McClary slapped his sheet of paper down on the desk and scowled at Lindsay.

"Ms. Robinson," he said crisply. "That sort of behavior won't be tolerated here. I'll have to ask that you excuse yourself from this class for the day."

A murmured gasp went through the room. None of the girls had ever been *kicked out* of class before. Shiva-Rose was startled; maybe the man really did have it in for Lindsay.

If Lindsay was rattled, though, she didn't show it. She merely rose up in her platform sandals, slung her Alexander McQueen for Target tote bag over one shoulder, and strode across the room as if it were her personal runway.

She made a point of slamming the door behind her.

"Shiva-Rose."

Acting class was finally over, and Shiva-Rose, drained and fighting back tears, turned at the sound of her name.

Mack was waiting outside the classroom, leaning against the wall, looking as handsome as ever.

Shiva-Rose's pulse rate skyrocketed. During the first session at TMP, Mack had flirted with her so much that she'd finally relented and spent a fun day with him exploring the city, trying to ignore the fact of his being a teacher at the program. (Unlike Alexis, Shiva-Rose was a rule-follower.) But then Mack had revealed to her that he was only eighteen, and she had felt safer around him. She'd started to trust him. Until their last encounter, when he'd basically tried to make her cheat on the photo shoot challenge. Shiva-Rose had declined, and they hadn't spoken since. But her skin had caught fire when she saw him yesterday at Del Posto. And now that they were standing so close she felt her willpower begin to crumble.

"Hi there," he added, giving her a small smile. His voice was raspy, jagged. It unsettled her every time. In the best possible way. "Can I see you for a minute?"

She shook her head and started to walk away—*this is wrong, this is wrong!*—but he touched her arm, and just like that, all her senses went into hyperdrive.

"It'll just take a sec, promise," Mack said.

Shiva-Rose glanced around. In the hallway, girls were dispersing, reapplying lip gloss, heading for lunch, and debating whether McClary was a jerk or a genius.

Some of the girls, Alexis and Chloe especially, had shone in the acting exercises. The first one, which McClary pompously called the "Puppy Monologue" *was* babyish, but after that they moved on to improvisation. McClary had assigned them different animals to act out. Alexis had been all energy, and Chloe had been pure grace. Shiva-Rose had stammered like an idiot and tripped over her own two feet, missed her cues, and basically, as she'd feared, made a fool of herself.

She wasn't the only girl who struggled (although she was the one who struggled most), and McClary had shown no mercy. He'd scolded her, mimicked her poorly read lines, and essentially told Shiva-Rose she had no chops whatsoever.

Confirming what Shiva-Rose had already suspected.

She would never be an actress.

But now the trauma of the whole experience seemed to melt away as she stood facing Mack. Shiva-Rose was keenly aware that if she continued to stand there with him, some of the girls would notice the photo instructor getting cozy with his favorite subject.

"Come on," she said at last, gesturing to an empty classroom. Hoping no one saw them, she ducked inside the room and Mack followed.

She'd talk to him. Fine. But she wouldn't look at him. He'd see her sorrowful expression. And she'd fall into his piercing green eyes. Eyes that matched hers in intensity.

"What's going on?" Mack demanded, taking a

step closer to Shiva-Rose. "You haven't answered my calls — are you avoiding me?"

Shiva-Rose didn't reply, keeping her gaze firmly on her silver Converse sneakers.

Mack rested a light hand on her arm. "Are you okay? You look upset."

"No," she lied unconvincingly. "It was just . . . a tough class."

"Tell me about it." His voice softened, he was all tenderness. Shiva-Rose couldn't resist. She looked up, and into his beautiful eyes. He smiled at her. She hated that she was going to tell him, couldn't make herself not tell him. So it all came spilling out, how she'd flubbed the acting class, how McClary had mocked her.

"That's not an appropriate way for a teacher to behave," he said.

Neither is this, thought Shiva-Rose. But his company was like a balm to her bruised ego. She could only shake her head.

"Well, it was only one class," he said soothingly.

"But McClary will be judging the final audition! He'll have a say in who wins or loses the challenge."

Mack gave her a silky smile. "Yes, but so will I."

"I don't want any special consideration," Shiva-Rose said firmly. "I mean that, Mack. And besides, it's not like it's going to be subjective. My performance will be bad by anybody's standards. If you give me anything other than a D, it will look like you're showing favoritism."

Mack shrugged, but thankfully, he didn't argue.

"Forget about the class," he said dismissively. "Forget the commercial. It's trite. Anyone can do that. You are the most arrestingly beautiful girl in the competition. In fact, those pictures I shot of you on the ferry came out great. I'm thinking of selling them."

"No," said Shiva-Rose. "It's against the rules. No one is allowed to do anything on a professional level until the contest is over."

"I know, but . . ."

"I don't want to break the rules, Mack. Just like I didn't want to cheat in the last challenge."

"But you said I could submit them. . . ."

"You promised to wait until after the summer, when the Top Model program is over," she reminded him.

"I lied." Mack grinned, his eyes sparkling. Why did he have to be so *cute*?

"Well, unsubmit them," Shiva-Rose snapped. "I take back my permission. You can't use them." She glared at him.

Mack sighed. "Okay. We'll wait till summer's over. I'll withdraw the submission. I promise."

Then he reached for her hand, and Shiva-Rose gave in — she intertwined her fingers with his. They smiled at each other, and just like that, all her worry and anger seemed to evaporate.

"I should go," she said after a minute, not wanting the charged moment between them to go on for much longer.

"All right," Mack said reluctantly. "Maybe we can have dinner this week?"

"Maybe," Shiva-Rose replied noncommittally, not wanting Mack to see the happiness in her eyes. Spending more time with the soulful photographer was all she wanted to do.

She waved good-bye and walked off down the hall, feeling her thoughts whirl.

This was bad.

She was falling for Mack. And she had no idea what to do about it.

CHAPTER FIVE
BLIND ITEM

Alexis had never been on a shopping spree before. She'd been on a shop*lifting* spree, certainly. But something told her this experience was going to be vastly different.

As she and her roommates walked up Madison Avenue toward the renowned shopping paradise called Barneys—prompting, as they always did, appreciative stares from passing boys—Alexis couldn't seem to wipe the goofy grin off her face. She'd been smiling the whole subway ride uptown, ignoring her roommates' snarky chitchat. Finally, for the first time in days, she was feeling calm and centered again. She'd won the first challenge fair and square, and now she was going to reward herself with five thousand dollars worth of high-end treasure! And for once in her life she could do it *without* having to wonder where the security cameras were positioned.

"So Barneys is a kind of a big deal, huh?" Alexis asked as they waited for the WALK signal to appear so they could cross Sixtieth Street.

"Barneys is what Macy's wants to be when it grows up," Lindsay explained. "They sell nothing but the best of the best."

"I checked out their Web site — they have every designer you could dream of," Shiva-Rose added.

"They sell *class*," Chloe put in importantly.

Alexis rolled her eyes, catching Chloe's inference: *You* could use all the class you can get.

Alexis wondered how much class she could purchase with five grand, then chuckled to herself. Probably not as much as she could steal.

The thought knocked the chuckle right out of her. After what happened the other night, she was feeling a lot less confident about her criminal capabilities.

If her roomies were at all concerned about Alexis's felonious tendencies on this trip, they weren't saying. They were accompanying her on the shopping spree for one reason: exposure. In her scant time at Top Model Prep, Alexis had learned that exposure to a model is like oxygen.

Since Alexis's shopping escapade was going to be photographed and written up in *Seventeen* magazine, the others wanted in on it, too.

"We're here," Lindsay announced.

Alexis stopped dead in her tracks and stared at the building, rising up out of Madison Avenue as if it had grown there. The windows of the ground floor were bedecked with simple, slanting red awnings, and for a moment, Alexis had the crazy feeling that the store was sticking its tongue (or tongues) out at her.

Victoria Devachan greeted Alexis, Lindsay, Chloe, and Shiva-Rose as the uniformed doorman ushered the girls in through the main door. Their imposing headmistress was flanked by a trendy-looking young woman — the *Seventeen* features editor, Alexis guessed — and a balding guy with a camera who was clearly the photographer. Also in attendance was a small horde of local news reporters and cameramen, and, of course, the immaculately clad Barneys salespeople.

The plan was for Alexis to just shop to her heart's content (assuming her heart could be made content on a five thousand dollar budget) and the *Seventeen* people would record it all for posterity. She'd pose in designer duds and gaze giddily at her reflection in dressing room mirrors while her roommates hovered in the background, looking encouraging and helpful.

The local reporters took a few shots, asked a few questions, then peaced-out. All except one.

A paunchy, mustachioed guy stepped up to Victoria and thrust a copy of one of the New York City tabloids (the one by which he himself was employed, according to his press pass) under her chin. Victoria shrank away from the tabloid pages instinctively, as if the very ink were poisonous (which, metaphorically at least, it certainly could be). Out of the corner of her eye, Alexis noticed one of the salespeople flinch.

"Do you have a comment about this?" the reporter asked in a gravelly voice, opening to the middle of the newspaper and pointing to a secondary headline on the page.

Victoria read the bold type of the headline. Her face turned ashen as her eyes darted over the brief article. Alexis read along:

FASHION DISASTER

Top Model Prep, known for teaching model wannabes the art of catwalking and lip-lining, has apparently expanded its curriculum to include another more useful, albeit less glamorous, skill: shoplifting. The recent winner of the program's first "challenge" was caught taking a "five-finger discount" at the Max Brenner chocolate shop. This reporter wonders if TMP plans to hire Winona Ryder to teach the Advanced Course.

Alexis felt trembles all down her body. Her heart dropped to her recently shoplifted Stuart Weitzman ballet flats.

No.

Who had done this?

"A blind item," Lindsay muttered. "That's what they call a little blurb of information when there's no source, and no names are given."

A blind item, Alexis thought. In this case, you'd have to be blind, deaf, and dumb not to know who the little snippet referred to.

Or who had planted it. Alexis narrowed her eyes at Lindsay.

Victoria hesitated only a second before pretending to laugh it off. "Pure fabrication," she said, with a dismissive wave of her perfectly manicured hand. "But you know what they say: You're nobody until somebody lies about you." She placed a firm — *very* firm — arm around Alexis's shoulders and went on. "Honestly, these tabloid writers are getting truly desperate for stories if they've resorted to making up lies about innocent *students*. I mean, really . . . it must be a particularly slow week for gossip. Paris Hilton must be under house arrest."

The onlookers laughed and the reporter skulked off. Victoria's arm lingered a moment longer around Alexis's shoulder, and the message was clear: We *will* discuss this later. Then Victoria stalked off to go chat with the features editor. Alexis wrung her hands, wondering what her fate would be.

Alexis was surprised to feel Shiva-Rose lean in close to her. "Shake it off," she advised in a whisper. "Remember why you're here."

Alexis nodded, taking a deep breath. Putting the blind item out of her head, she allowed herself to take her first good look around the store.

It was amazing! Part retail space, part country club. The place actually *smelled* exclusive, as if the air-conditioning were being piped in directly from heaven. Alexis noticed her roommates all gazing about in rapture. Even Chloe, who'd been raised in the lap of this particular brand of luxury, seemed impressed by the cool, imposing glamour of the place.

"I've been to Barneys in Beverly Hills," she said, reverently running her finger along the top of a pristine glass display case, "but this is just different somehow."

"Where should I start?" Alexis wondered aloud.

"How about Fred's?" Lindsay suggested. "I'm starving."

"Who's Fred?" Alexis asked.

"It's the restaurant upstairs," Lindsay explained knowingly, as if she'd eaten there a million times. "But you'll probably blow your entire five grand before you get past the appetizers."

"The restaurant is called *Fred's*?" Shiva-Rose couldn't help emitting a little snort of laughter. "Fred. And Barney. That's hilarious."

Alexis gave her a blank look.

"You know," said Shiva-Rose. "Fred and Barney. Like on *The Flintstones*!"

Lindsay rolled her eyes. "Is that what people *do* where you're from?" She sneered. "Sit around and watch reruns of lame old TV shows?"

"Yes, as matter of fact it is," Shiva-Rose shot back smoothly. "Which is why *Yes, We Blend* is such a hit."

Lindsay looked ready to break the arm off the nearest mannequin and smack Shiva-Rose over the head with it.

"C'mon!" said Chloe, suddenly linking her arm in Alexis's. "Let's shop!"

Laughing as Chloe tugged her toward the escalator, Alexis couldn't help but wonder if the arm link was a genuine sign of friendship or simply a show for the cameras. Truth be told, she didn't care. Not now. Because when the next issue of *Seventeen* hit the newsstands, she, Alexis Cournos, of miserable pathetic little Hamtramck High, would be featured there in its glossy, glamorous pages, kickin' it with glossy, glamorous Chloe Huntley, shopping at Barneys, eating at Fred's!

She had five Gs burning a hole in her stolen Gucci bag, and it was time for her to spend them.

At the end of the day, Alexis found herself the proud owner of one pair of Citizens of Humanity skinny jeans, one powder blue Balenciaga change purse (she had no idea why, but maybe she'd give it to her grandmother), and one dangly pair of Cathy Waterman earrings that registered a 9.9 on the bling scale and ate up nearly two of her five thousand bucks.

She also bought four pairs of wraparound Oliver Peoples sunglasses — one pair for herself and matching pairs for each of her roommates. The girls had declined politely, at first, but Alexis sweetly insisted. "They can be like our own version of friendship bracelets," she'd said, specifically for the *Seventeen* editor to hear, and, more important, to jot down.

Alexis knew she had a naïve side, but she could be as cunning as the best of them.

Lindsay glanced cynically at the $375 price tag. "Nobody's *that* good of a friend," she muttered, but she put the trendy sunglasses on anyway.

Victoria beamed at Alexis's generosity, gushing, for the benefit of the *Seventeen* editor, about the spirit of camaraderie at Top Model Prep, and the public's unfounded belief that the modeling world was cutthroat and competitive. Here was living proof that the TMP girls were forging profound and lasting friendships. Sisterhood, baby. Girl power.

Yeah. Right.

Alexis also purchased three pastel Lacoste polo shirts for her brother, Nick, on the outside chance that the juvenile detention facility in which he was presently incarcerated suddenly decided to jump on the preppy-chic bandwagon. It made her a little queasy to think of spending even a single penny of her hard-won cash on him, but it was what it was. Prize money, hush money. Same thing.

The whole time, the photographer had digitally captured the shopping-slash-bonding experience and the features editor had scribbled notes for her article, including a quote from Alexis: *"The best part about the whole day was sharing it with my friends. In my book, we're all winners!"*

At those words, Shiva-Rose bit back a chuckle. Lindsay pointed her finger into her mouth, pretending to make herself throw up. And Chloe stood off to the side, checking her phone for text messages from Liam and totally not paying attention.

Bonding time was officially *over*.

That afternoon, he was waiting for her at Bethesda Fountain. Cliché, she knew, touristy in the extreme. But ever since she'd read about the spot in her guidebook, there was just something so romantic and old-fashioned about it that Alexis had suggested they meet there for their date.

Their date.

She still felt like pinching herself when she thought about it. She had never been anyone's girlfriend or even potential girlfriend before, and secretly she feared that for the rest of her life her Facebook status would be locked on "single." Single! Not even "it's complicated"; she would have settled for that. But now, it seemed as if the Dating Gods were smiling on her and not only was she well on her way to being "in a relationship," but in a relationship with the absolute sweetest, most sensitive and, oh, did she mention . . . *gorgeous* guy on the planet.

Seeing Shane Cooper perched on the rim of the fountain with the sun in his hair made Alexis's heart quicken. He smiled when he saw her. Alexis was certain the temperature in Central Park rose twenty degrees when the corners of that full mouth turned upward.

And that Shane was even more dazzling than the carved angel that rose above the fountain.

"Hi," she said, accepting his hug. He was wearing a vintage Elvis Costello T-shirt, battered cargo shorts, and olive-green Havaianas.

"Hey." He drew back and looked at her. "Nice earrings."

Alexis giggled, touching the glam Cathy Watermans. "Yeah, I know they're a little much for a walk in the park. But I just got them this morning, and I couldn't wait to wear them."

Shane smiled again, as if he thought she was the most adorable thing ever.

But on that front, he would be wrong, because, without a doubt, hands down, no contest, *he* was definitely the most adorable thing ever—as evidenced by the fact that at that very moment he was bending down to pick up a huge picnic basket.

Alexis's eyes widened with delight. "A picnic? You brought us a picnic?"

"Yeah." Shane's cheeks went a little red (*beyond* adorable) and he shrugged. "Too corny?"

"Not at all!" A picnic in Central Park was off-the-charts romantic.

Shane hoisted the basket onto his hip, then took her hand lightly in his and led her to a grassy spot under an enormous tree. Alexis watched as he opened the basket and removed a big, square, red-and-white checkered tablecloth that he spread carefully on the ground. Then he withdrew four plastic take-out containers, two sandwiches wrapped in deli paper, and two bottles of Evian.

"Models live on this stuff," he joked, indicating the water.

She winked at him. "You oughta know."

Next out of the picnic hamper came a handful of paper napkins, two plastic forks, his iPod (nestled into a battery-operated speaker, ready to serenade them), and a family-size bag of salt-and-vinegar chips.

Had she mentioned to him that they were her favorite? Yes. And he'd remembered. She could have thrown her arms around him; instead, she reached for the bag of potato chips, tore it open, and popped one in her mouth.

"Okay, so . . . we've got coleslaw"—Shane tapped the cover of each take-out container in turn—"pasta salad with pesto, pasta salad *without* pesto, and German potato salad."

"You're a big fan of the side dish, I see," Alexis teased.

"Very big fan. *Love* the side dish." Shane's eyes twinkled as he picked up one of the sandwiches. "And here we've got turkey on whole wheat with lettuce, tomato, and mayonnaise. I figured you can't go wrong with a classic, right?"

"True." Alexis crunched another chip and nodded with mock seriousness, then pointed to the second sandwich. "What's that one?"

"That one? That one's liverwurst and tongue on rye bread with raw onion."

Alexis's mouth dropped in horror and Shane laughed. "Kidding! I'm kidding." He reached over and gently tapped her chin upward to close her mouth. "It's roast beef and Swiss with Thousand Island dressing."

Alexis was visibly relieved, which made him laugh even harder.

"You'll have to learn to be a little less gullible," he said, unwrapping the turkey sandwich and handing her half, "if you're gonna make it in this business."

"I guess so." Alexis took a bite of the sandwich. "I mean, I think I'd do just about anything to make it as a model . . . but the one thing I would definitely *not* do is eat liverwurst." She grinned.

Shane swallowed a bite of the roast beef sandwich and gave her a concerned look. "Almost anything, huh?"

"Well, yeah. Being a model means a lot to me." *More than you could ever know,* she added silently. "Is that a bad thing?"

Shane considered the question, gathering up a forkful of pasta salad. "It could be. It's a tough business."

Feeling flirty, Alexis leaned toward him and put her hand on his muscular arm. "You don't seem any worse for wear," she said in a silky voice.

"That's because I don't take it seriously." He smiled, clearly enjoying the way her hand lingered gently on his wrist. "For me, it's just a means to an end. A summer job." He reached over and pushed a stray curl away from her face. "I just don't want to see you get hurt."

The sincerity of his words flooded her heart with warmth. "What do you mean?"

"Well, right now, you're competing against . . . what? Thirty, forty girls?"

Alexis nodded.

"In the real world . . . that is, if you can call the modeling world 'real,' the numbers are a lot higher. Like, for some jobs you might be up against a hundred girls. And all one hundred of them want the job, *need* the job, just as badly you do."

"Badly enough to eat liverwurst?" Alexis asked coyly, hoping to bring back the playful mood.

"Badly enough to do just about anything. It's crazy, Lex. The amount of rejection . . . it's just nuts. You can get rejected from one job because your hair is too curly, and the next day you'll get rejected from a different job because your hair is too straight. Maybe you're too ethnic-looking for the *Teen Vogue* cover, but for the *Lucky* cover you're not ethnic-looking enough. Too tall, too short. Too many highlights, not enough highlights . . . your eyebrows are wrong, your teeth are too white, your agent fought with the client . . . whatever. More often than not, the answer is a big fat nonnegotiable no."

"Wow." Alexis frowned. So far what she'd seen of the industry had been a mixed bag. Sure, Lindsay was conniving and snarky, but the others had been mostly okay. Look how Chloe had come to her rescue at Max Brenner. And today, shopping together at Barneys had actually been fun. She had begun to feel as though she'd made some friends here. Her best friend being that five thousand dollar check, of course. "Is it really that horrible?" she asked.

"Not always. I mean, sometimes you're exactly what they're looking for, and the next thing you know you're on a billboard in lower Manhattan wearing nothing but a pair of Calvin Klein tighty-whities and a smile."

He put his hands on her shoulders, rested his forehead against hers. "But it could take a long time to get there. I just want you to understand that."

"Thank you." She hadn't meant to whisper, but the words came out soft and breathy, like a kiss.

A kiss. He was touching her cheek, coaxing her lips closer to his. . . .

Her first kiss . . .

"Shane? Dude! I thought that was you!"

Kiss . . . canceled.

Shane turned around, leaving Alexis with her eyes closed and her lips half parted. It took her a moment to come out of her minitrance. When she finally opened her eyes, she saw Shane standing on his feet, high-fiving a guy who was almost—*almost*—as drop-dead gorgeous as he was.

"Graham, this is Alexis," Shane said. "The girl I told you about."

The thought of Shane telling someone about her sent a giddy shiver down Alexis's spine. The sensation wasn't quite as good as the kiss had promised to be, but it was close enough.

Shane continued the introductions. "Lex, this is my friend, Graham. I guess you could say we work together. We've got the same agent."

Alexis smiled up at Graham. Physically, he was the complete antithesis of Shane, who was dark, smoldering, rugged. Graham had the sort of "teen idol" looks that made little girls swoon. He was athletically built, but slender, with straight blond hair and gray eyes. His incongruously dark eyelashes would do any female supermodel proud, and his dimples, Alexis was certain, would one day be legendary.

"Nice to meet you," said Alexis.

Graham flashed his perfect smile. "Hey, are you gonna finish that sandwich? Cuz I'm starved."

"Oh . . . uh . . ." Alexis shrugged. "Here." She handed Graham the untouched half of the turkey sandwich, which he devoured in two bites.

Shane rolled his eyes, but he was grinning. Apparently, it didn't take long for Graham to feel comfortable around someone new.

"Man, that was *awe*some," said Graham, helping himself to a handful of chips. "I love tuna salad."

Alexis looked at him. "Um . . . that was turkey."

"Yeah, I know," said Graham, picking a kalamata olive out of the pasta salad. "I'm just sayin'. I *love* tuna salad." He popped the olive into his mouth. "And you know what else is good? Pastrami. Pastrami is *awe*some. Right?"

"Welcome to my world," Shane whispered into Alexis's ear, then he surprised her by planting a sweet, soft kiss on her cheek.

"I think I like your world," she whispered back.

"Good. Stay as long as you like."

"You know what else is good?" Graham was saying. "That movie. *Slumdog Millionaire*. That was, like, so good. Right?" He smiled at Alexis, then turned to Shane. "Dude, pass the coleslaw."

Alexis couldn't help herself. She laughed out loud, certain that this would go down as the most ridiculous, most perfect date in the history of the world.

Perfect enough to make her forget about that annoying blind item. For now.

CHAPTER SIX
BUBBLE HEADS

Chloe, Shiva-Rose, and Lindsay sat in the common room of 14C, all of them staring eagerly at the giant, beautifully wrapped gift box on the coffee table. For the past twenty minutes, they'd been holding the exact same pose, which Chloe found sort of funny. As if they were waiting for someone to take their picture.

"When is Alexis going to come back already?" Lindsay groused. "She better not be stealing stuff again."

"I think she's meeting that guy, Shane?" Chloe offered, remembering something Alexis had said that morning, and Shiva-Rose nodded. "I'm glad," Chloe added, feeling generous. "It would be good for her to have a boyfriend, considering everything that's happened. Right?"

Before the other girls could respond, the front door opened and in walked Alexis, her glowing face and dreamy eyes confirming Chloe's sentiments. Clearly, her afternoon with Shane had gone very well. Chloe was curious to hear details — now that things seemed to be back on with Liam, she wanted the whole world to be in love.

"It's about time!" Lindsay cried, jumping up. "We've been waiting for you so we could open this thing! Not that we were being polite or anything. The rules say we all have to open it together." With that, she marched across the hall and knocked on the door of 14A. Seconds later, Ava, Jana, and Faye swarmed into the common room of 14C. They, too, gawked at the gift-wrapped box.

Alexis blinked, confused. "What's going on?"

"It's our first 'V-mail,'" Shiva-Rose explained. "From Victoria. It came about an hour ago."

Lindsay flung herself onto the sofa and stared at the box like she was Indiana Jones and it was the Ark of the Covenant. "The waiting was killing me!"

Chloe groaned, annoyed by Lindsay's dramatics. "Well, we're all here now. Open it already."

That was all the encouragement Lindsay needed. She tore into the wrapping and opened the box.

And let out a shriek of epic proportions.

"Whoa!" Shiva-Rose covered her ears with her hands. "What's in there anyway? A Jonas brother?"

Chloe laughed, thinking that Liam was cuter than any Jonas.

"Better!" cried Lindsay, digging into the box and whipping out article after article of deluxe clothing. There were scarves, skinny jeans, buttery leather jackets, and fluttery dresses.

Alexis, clearly still lost in thoughts of her afternoon with Shane, was only vaguely aware of the magenta pashmina that landed on her head. She pushed the fringe out of her eyes. "Clothes?"

"Clothes," Chloe deadpanned. "Wow. That's amazing. I mean, 'cause it's not like we get to dress up in designer fashions every single minute of our lives here at TMP or anything."

"Not in these we don't," gushed Lindsay, holding up a wrap dress in a safari print and hugging it to her as though it were a long-lost relative. "These are Kitty Lyons."

Faye's eyes lit up. "No *way*!"

Lindsay pointed to the label on the inside of the dress. "Way!"

"Who's Kitty Lyons?" Alexis and Shiva-Rose asked in unison. Chloe opened her mouth to answer, but naturally Lindsay beat her to it.

"A new designer," Lindsay explained. "No, *the* new designer. Her clothes aren't even available in the United States yet, but everyone is dying to get them. I heard Jennifer Aniston had to practically beg Kitty to loan her that gray pencil skirt and satin ruffle blouse she wore to Drew Barrymore's birthday party." She fished a scaly-looking miniskirt out of the box. "Oh! Snakeskin is *so* me!"

That's because you're a viper, Chloe thought. "So what are these clothes for anyway?" she asked, disinterested.

Shiva-Rose was already opening the envelope that had come with the box. "They're for us to wear to a party," she said, pulling the thick cream-colored card from the envelope. "A launch party, to be exact, for the new Kitty Lyons collection. This Friday night."

This elicited a shriek from Lindsay, followed by a cacophony of shouts and giggles from Alexis, Shiva-Rose, and the girls from 14A.

Chloe didn't exactly shout, but she did smile. The party was Friday.

Liam could be her date!

Together—the senator's son, the diva's daughter—they would be the focus of every paparazzi in the place, and even before the party was over, images of the dazzling young couple—holding hands, dancing close, snuggling in a corner booth—would be splashed across the Internet, so that everyone could see how very much in love they were.

Take that, Juliet Rivers.

Take that, Lindsay.

The next morning, the thirty remaining girls chatted excitedly about the upcoming launch party as they made their way to their classes. Today's class was Acting Technique. Chloe was looking forward to it, but as she sauntered into the classroom alongside Shiva-Rose, she sensed her roommate's fear and dread.

Chloe made an effort to comfort the girl. "At least Robert McClary won't be teaching us this time," she murmured. She knew Shiva-Rose simply could not bear further humiliation at the hands of that pompous jerk.

"Did he quit?" Shiva-Rose asked hopefully.

"No, but I overheard Victoria saying he was 'taking a meeting' with some Broadway producer today, so he wouldn't be here."

"Taking a meeting, huh?" Shiva-Rose held the classroom door open for Chloe. "I wish he were taking the first flight out of JFK instead."

The girls shared a smile, and filed into the classroom, where rows of chairs had been set up.

Lindsay had already seated herself in the first row, dead center, just behind a video camera that stood on a tall tripod. Chloe and Shiva-Rose sat behind her, and soon all the girls from 14A and 14C had straggled in.

Moments later, Dan'yel and Anabelle arrived.

"Good morning," chirped Dan'yel as Anabelle began passing out script pages. "Welcome to Commercial Auditioning 101. Yes, I know we're not talking about theater or even film work here. But before you go copping an elitist 'tude on me, just take a moment to consider this. Some of the most memorable snippets of pop culture—catchphrases, jingles, characters—originated in television commercials. For instance, my entire generation was obsessed with inquiring 'Where's the Beef?' Can anyone give me a more current example?"

Faye raised her hand. "The cell phone commercial where the guy keeps asking, 'Can you hear me now?'"

Chloe smiled to herself, putting one hand on the iPhone that sat snugly in the pocket of her denim mini. *Her* cell phone was like her lifeline—it connected her to Liam.

Dan'yel nodded. "Yes. We've all used that one, haven't we? What else?"

Jana shouted out, "Wassup?" and everyone laughed.

Lindsay posed the perennial question, "Got Milk?"

"What about the Energizer Bunny?" offered Alexis.

Fitting, thought Chloe. The girl could be just as hyperactive as the drum-pounding bunny.

"He's an icon," Dan'yel conceded. "So you see . . . while no one could ever mistake any of these examples for high art, they do have a place in our collective consciousness, and, in some cases, our hearts. Now, the question is . . . who among you will become the next Brooke Shields, telling the world that nothing comes between her and her Calvin Kleins?"

Chloe, of course, got the reference. Brooke Shields was a close friend of her mother's; they'd modeled together a million times, back in the day. A few true supermodel-trivia buffs laughed at the teacher's allusion to the controversial 1980 TV ad, but most of the girls missed the joke entirely.

"Oh, just look it up on YouTube," said Dan'yel, rolling his eyes. "Now, moving on . . ."

"I've handed out a commercial script," Anabelle explained. "Your real audition material for the actual Mane Event commercial is still being tweaked by the advertising agency. I promise you, however, you will have it in advance in order to prepare for the challenge. For now, we'll just practice with this one, which happens to be for a fictional shampoo brand."

Chloe glanced down at the script. Whoever had written it had named the make-believe product Bubble Head. Well, in this crowd, she thought wryly, the term wasn't entirely inappropriate.

Lindsay raised her hand. "Actually, sometimes commercial scripts include little cartoon sketches, a miniature storyboard, showing the commercial shot by shot." She turned to give the group a smug smile. "I know because when I was much younger, back before my big break on *Yes, We Blend*, I did several commercials."

Can't she just be eliminated today? Chloe thought.

"That's right!" said Faye. "I remember seeing you in the commercial for that baby doll. You know, the one that when you pressed her little belly button she'd throw up! Oh, what was she called again? Baby Barfs A Lot?"

Lindsay shook her head, scowling. "The doll's *name*," she snapped, "was Tammy Tummy-ache, and she came with an itty-bitty bottle of pretend Pepto-Bismol that was actually real lip gloss."

Right, thought Chloe. Makes perfect sense. Because the first thing an infant wants to do after she pukes is touch up her lip color. God, this was becoming surreal. All she wanted to do was go off alone and write a poem, maybe a thousand poems, to express the way she was feeling. She wanted to send those poems to Liam, to let him see the side of her that only he appreciated. But no. She was trapped here, with Lindsay and her gigantic ego, with Bubble Head and "Can you hear me now?" and the frickin' Energizer Bunny.

Liam, she thought, her heart aching. She couldn't wait to see him. It had been much too long.

"If memory serves," Dan'yel was saying, "I do believe that Tammy Tummy-ache was recalled almost immediately by the manufacturer when her reusable vomit was found to be, in fact, toxic."

"There was only one lawsuit," Lindsay grumbled in a huff, "and they settled out of court."

Anabelle sighed. "Thank you, Lindsay. Now, if I may continue . . . the lines you will be reading are designed to make the consumer believe that her life simply will not be complete until she has washed her hair with"—she consulted the page in her hand—"with Bubble Head–brand shampoo. Now, take a moment to look at the lines, and then we'll have a few of you volunteer to do a cold read."

The room went quiet as the girls dived into the script, which was little more than a paragraph in length. Chloe wondered if Jana would need

SparkNotes, then mentally scolded herself for being mean-spirited.

"I'm ready." Lindsay's voice broke the silence. "I volunteer to go first."

Dan'yel sighed, looking as if he'd expected as much. "Thank you, Lindsay."

Lindsay went to stand in front of the camera and gave a shake of her luscious dark hair. Chloe had to hand it to her, the girl had poise. Confidence oozed out of every pore. She didn't even look at the script — she'd memorized it that quickly.

"Would I trust this hair to just any shampoo?" Lindsay practically sang the question, flashing her eyes at the camera. Energy pulsed from her. "No way! Bubble Head is packed with vitamins, amino acids, and . . ." She paused, leaning toward the camera as though she wanted to kiss it. ". . . our own *secret* blend of natural botanicals to give you the shiniest, silkiest hair imaginable."

Then she finished up with a near-acrobatic toss of her head, smiling beautifully as her shimmering curls swung softly back into place.

Chloe hated to admit it, but she was totally impressed. Lindsay's performance wasn't Shakespeare-caliber, but it was exactly what a shampoo commercial was supposed to be. The Bubble Head execs (if Bubble Head execs actually existed) would be jumping for joy and shouting "Ka-*ching*!" and Lindsay most likely would become the spokesmodel for Bubble Head shampoo, perhaps even be dubbed "The Bubble Head Girl." There would definitely be a certain poetic justice in that, Chloe realized, but alas, Bubble Head shampoo, like Bubble Head execs, did not actually exist.

"That was fabulous," said Dan'yel. "Really, quite, quite good."

Anabelle pressed her hand to her heart. "I am utterly compelled at this moment to lather, rinse, and repeat! Well done."

Lindsay sauntered — yes, sauntered — back to her seat. Baby Upchuck (or whatever she was called) was all but forgotten now.

After Lindsay had taken her seat (and her metaphorical bow), Dan'yel spoke a little about diction and enunciation. He explained that clearly pronouncing the first and last letter of every word would keep the speech from sounding garbled. "Words are like people," he said. "They need their space." He talked about inflection and "punching" certain, significant words for emphasis. Oh, and smiling. *Smile. Smile!*

Chloe couldn't help but think of her mother, who, like any good supermodel, had always urged Chloe to smile through everything.

Ugh.

Some of the girls asked questions, while others made notes on their script pages. Chloe didn't bother. She was suddenly engrossed in two very different types of writing. One was a text from her mother; the other a text from Liam.

Mom's read:

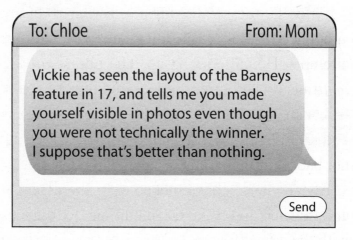

To: Chloe   From: Mom

Vickie has seen the layout of the Barneys feature in 17, and tells me you made yourself visible in photos even though you were not technically the winner. I suppose that's better than nothing.

Send

Chloe pressed DELETE as hard as she could, then focused on Liam's text.

To: Chloe   From: Liam

I'll be there Friday night. Can't wait to see you baby. I miss having you in my arms.

Send

Chloe had to stop herself from letting out a squeal of pure joy. Up until this moment, she hadn't been positive Liam would actually show. Now it seemed as if their long-overdue reunion was going to happen.

Chloe's attention was diverted when Dan'yel announced that he was ready to see more audition attempts. He called Jana up. The phrase *amino acids* nearly killed her, and she didn't have much luck with *botanicals,* either. She did smile though, and she copied Lindsay's hair shake. All in all, not bad.

Faye went next, but didn't do well. She stuttered and fidgeted and had trouble making eye contact with the camera.

Alexis got points for her enthusiasm, but Dan'yel noted that her Midwest drawl was a problem. The same went for Shiva-Rose's Israeli accent. Just as Shiva-Rose had feared, she was a mess when it came to acting. The more she stumbled, the more nervous she became until Chloe feared the poor girl might pull a Tammy Tummy-ache and puke all over the place. Mercifully, Dan'yel let Shiva-Rose sit down. Chloe was watching Ava practice her hair flip when her iPhone buzzed again; another text from Mom.

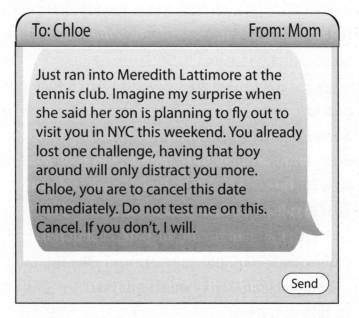

To: Chloe   From: Mom

Just ran into Meredith Lattimore at the tennis club. Imagine my surprise when she said her son is planning to fly out to visit you in NYC this weekend. You already lost one challenge, having that boy around will only distract you more. Chloe, you are to cancel this date immediately. Do not test me on this. Cancel. If you don't, I will.

Send

What? No! Chloe didn't remember buying a ticket for this emotional roller-coaster ride, but there she was, plummeting toward misery, heading for the loop-the-loop of absolute fury. Her stomach was in knots, and she didn't know whether to scream or weep. Could Charlotte really do this to her?

Of course she could. Charlotte Huntley could do anything she wanted.

"Chloe?" Dan'yel beckoned her forward. "Your turn."

Chloe was shaking, but not from stage fright. She was livid and heartsick and desperate all at once.

But it was her turn. And the show—or in this case, the inane commercial—must go on. Her mother's threat loomed in her mind as she stood and made her way toward the front of the room. She was sure Dan'yel was remembering a Pantene commercial her mother had rocked back in the '80s, imploring the audience not to dislike her because she was gorgeous.

Please don't mention it, she willed Dan'yel telepathically. *Please don't bring it up.*

Miraculously, he didn't. He waited for Chloe to take her place before the camera, to hit her mark, as they said in the business. She took a deep breath, letting herself feel all her emotions at once.

And didn't smile.

Instead, she reached up and took hold of a slender strand of her trademark corn silk hair. Gently, slowly, she ran her fingers from the root to the tip, fixing a smoldering gaze on the camera. "Would I trust this hair to just any shampoo?" She didn't speak the words exactly; it was more like she purred them. "No way. . . ." She shook her head ever so slightly, then slowly and without ever taking her eyes off the camera, lowered herself to the floor. Dan'yel quickly tilted the camera on its perch, struggling to keep her in the frame. Chloe was stretched out on her back, face turned to the camera, speaking slowly, deliberately. "Bubble Head is packed with vitamins, amino acids, and our own"—she pressed her index finger to her lips in a shushing gesture—"*secret* blend of natural botanicals to give you the shiniest"—in a flash she sat bolt upright—"silkiest hair imaginable." Without warning, she sprang to her feet, took her head in her hands, and frantically ruffled her flaxen hair until it stood out in wild disarray. *Then* she smiled.

Cut.

Print.

Wow.

The class (with the exception of Lindsay) leaped to their feet and cheered. Dan'yel was fanning at himself with both hands as though he were caught in a sudden heat wave. Anabelle might have been cleansing her aura or adjusting her chakras. In any case, she looked thoroughly wowed.

The consensus was unanimous: Chloe was amazing. A risk-taker. A natural.

But oh, how she wished — *wished* — she weren't. Wished her mother hadn't sent her here, wished her mother would let her come home. Or at the very least, would let Liam come visit.

Chloe thought back to her mother's commercial once again.

Don't hate me because I'm beautiful . . .
. . . Hate me because I'm ruining my daughter's life.

As soon as class was over, Chloe lingered outside the classroom to write the most depressing text message of her life. It was going to cause her physical pain to hit the SEND button. But she would do it, she had to. Charlotte had decreed it.

Leaning against the wall in the corridor as the

rest of the model-hopefuls hurried out to enjoy the afternoon, Chloe let out a long sigh, and typed:

To: Liam   From: Chloe

> Liam, baby, I'm sooooo sorry but you can't come out this weekend. Mom's being a nightmare. Please understand.

Send

"Chloe?"

She looked up to see Alexis standing there, looking nervous. "Oh. Hey."

"I know you really got me out of a jam at the chocolate place," Alexis began, "but I was wondering if I could ask you another favor."

Chloe shrugged, her mind still on Liam. "Sure."

"Well, remember when that reporter showed Victoria the blind item about the shoplifting?"

Chloe nodded. "I'm pretty sure Lindsay was the one who leaked the info to that rag."

"Me, too," said Alexis. "But whatever. I can't worry about her right now. I've got a bigger problem." She took a deep breath. "Victoria wants to talk to me about it. Now. In her office."

"Oh." Chloe winced. "That doesn't sound good."

"Yeah. So I was wondering, since you know her so well, maybe you'd . . . I don't know . . . kind of . . . come with me?"

Chloe thought for a moment before she answered. The fact was, there was no harm in her helping Alexis. Maybe focusing her attention on someone else would help Chloe get her mind off her own troubles. "Okay," she said at last.

Alexis looked as though a huge weight had been removed from her shoulders. "Oh, wow. Thank you, Chloe. Thank you so much."

"But you've got to do something for me."

"Anything."

"A lot of kids I know back in LA are kind of messed up. Some of them steal. Some of them do stuff I don't even want to think about." Chloe put a friendly hand on Alexis's shoulder. "I'm not saying you're as bad as that, but, Alexis, it's pretty clear you've got a problem. And I have a feeling it can only get worse."

Chloe was surprised to see Alexis's wide green eyes filling with tears. She didn't think her words would have such a strong effect, but they clearly had. Her roommate's lovely freckled face managed to register anger, shock, fear, and then profound gratitude.

"I'll come with you to talk to Victoria," Chloe continued, "and I'll go along with whatever story you tell her. But you've got to promise me you're going to get help. Talk to someone. A professional."

The tears were rolling down Alexis's face now. She wiped at them with the back of her wrist and nodded hard. "I will," she said. "I promise."

"Okay," said Chloe. "C'mon. Let's go see Aunt Vickie."

Later, Chloe would look back at that moment and understand exactly what people meant when they said, "No good deed goes unpunished."

CHAPTER SEVEN
KEEPING THE PEACE

"Somehow, I survived."

Shiva-Rose gazed at Alexis, riveted by her roommate's recounting of her conversation with the inimitable Victoria Devachan.

The two model-hopefuls were seated at a small table in a Starbucks on Spring Street, sucking down light Frappuccinos. Twenty minutes before, Shiva-Rose had received a text from Alexis, asking her to meet up there for some modicum of privacy. Shiva-Rose, still worn out by the awful acting class that day, and still caught up in swirling thoughts about Mack, had been happy to get out of the apartment for some distraction. And Alexis had insisted on a neutral spot a safe distance from the Top Model Residence.

"Really, I just don't want Lindsay to hear all this." Alexis sighed, tugging on an auburn curl. "I know she's the one who planted that blind item.

But Chloe's cool. If it weren't for her, I'd probably be in jail—or expelled by now."

Alexis had already told Shiva-Rose, in detail, how Chloe had backed her up during the show-down with Victoria. Sitting in Victoria's imposing office, Alexis had managed to convince the head-mistress that it had all been a misunderstanding, and with Chloe there as a witness, the powerful former supermodel seemed to have no choice but to believe them both. Victoria sent them off with a stern warning that any future hint of misconduct would result in a thorough investigation, blah, blah, blah, and Alexis had sworn that that would not be necessary.

"Good for Chloe," Shiva-Rose said, taking a long sip of her frothy drink. Maybe she'd mis-judged the LA princess. "I have to say, I'm a little surprised. She usually seems so self-involved. But she's really been there for you."

Shiva-Rose felt a little surge of hope. She hated any sort of conflict, and she wondered if Lindsay might redeem herself soon as well. Maybe then the four roommates could actually live in peace and establish some semblance of a friendship.

Or was she just delusional?

Alexis nodded, her expression sober. "I know, it's crazy. I mean, when she said she'd help me, she seemed really genuine. At first, a part of me wanted to tell her to mind her own business. But then I realized that she wasn't judging, she was really trying to help."

Alexis expounded a little bit more on how she wanted to change her ways, and Shiva-Rose couldn't resist sneaking a glance down at her watch. She was enjoying a catch-up with Alexis, but she was also scheduled to have a video chat with her dad in ten minutes. She'd deliberately lugged her laptop along to Starbucks for that purpose. She hoped Alexis would leave soon, because Shiva-Rose would much rather talk to her dad in private — if a crowded coffee shop in SoHo could be considered private.

Finally, Alexis announced that she had to call Shane. She thanked Shiva-Rose for listening, tossed out her empty Venti cup, and headed out into the hot city night.

Instantly, Shiva-Rose took out her laptop and went online. She signed into her account and seconds later she was looking into a familiar pair of warm, brown eyes.

Not her father's . . . Rahm's!

Shiva-Rose felt her heart somersault at the sight of her childhood friend, who, in recent years, had become just a tad bit crushworthy. What with all the Mack drama, she hadn't thought about Rahm in *forever*.

"Hey!" she cried, grinning at the computer screen. "What are you doing there?"

"Your dad invited me as a surprise." Rahm tilted his head, looking adorably nervous. "Hope it's okay."

"Okay? It's great!"

"So how's New York?"

Shiva-Rose beamed. "It's amazing! You can't even imagine. And the girls are actually not that bad. Oh, whoa, wait . . . guess who I'm rooming with! Lindsay Robinson."

From halfway around the world, Rahm's face registered shock. "The girl from *Yes, We Blend*? That's insane!"

"I know, right?" Shiva-Rose laughed.

"How are your classes?"

"Well, I like some better than others."

"And the teachers?"

Shiva-Rose swallowed hard. Visions of Mack's face, his alluring voice, flooded back to her. "Again . . . I like some better than others." She forced a chuckle.

"We miss you," Rahm said, then lowered his voice and said, "*I* miss you."

A little swirl of warmth unfurled in Shiva-Rose's stomach. Rahm had never said anything like that to her.

And she liked it.

"I miss you, too," she heard herself saying.

For a moment, they just looked at each other, across all those miles and oceans, until her father's voice off-camera broke the moment.

"My turn," he called happily, and slid into view beside Rahm. "How is my little girl doing all the way over there in the Big Apricot?"

Shiva-Rose laughed, but seeing her father brought a tightness to her throat. *Don't cry*, she told herself. "It's the Big Apple, Dad. And I'm fine. How are you?"

They talked and talked, catching up and trading anecdotes. Shiva-Rose forgot all about the Starbucks bustle around her as she was drawn back into her world at home. Together, her father and Rahm filled her in on all the things she was missing, everything from silly gossip about her cousins and friends to more important political issues. Shiva-Rose felt a stab of guilt for not keeping up with the news from Israel. It was easy to feel carefree here in New York, especially at TMP, where everyone's only objective seemed to be looking good and having fun.

Her father must have read her mind. "I'm glad you are having this summer to enjoy yourself," he said. "You are a young girl. You should be without worries. I am happy to see you happy."

A tear rolled down Shiva-Rose's cheek.

"But Rahm, here," her father went on, his voice taking on a teasing tone, "he is not so happy." He elbowed Rahm playfully in the ribs. "He comes over here all the time and stares at your window and wishes for you to come home."

Rahm laughed, but Shiva-Rose could see her guy friend was embarrassed.

"That's because you took my *Battlestar Galactica* DVD and I want it back," he teased.

They talked a while longer, then Shiva-Rose said she had to get back to the apartment. It was difficult to say good-bye.

Her father cleared his throat. "Sweetheart, I am sure I do not have to remind you that this coming Saturday . . ."

"I know, Dad," Shiva-Rose said. "I'll remember."

Her father nodded, collecting his thoughts, then gave her a brave smile. "Be a good girl," he said, a catch in his voice.

"I will." Shiva-Rose blew a kiss to the computer screen. "See you, Daddy. *Shalom.*"

Peace.

With a lump in her throat, Shiva-Rose closed her laptop, put it back into her messenger bag, and left Starbucks. Her thoughts full of her dad and Rahm and Mack and more, she walked out onto Spring Street. Slowly, she wound her way back to the Top Model Residence, apartment 14C. It wasn't home. But for now, it would have to be enough.

CHAPTER EIGHT
THE BIG NIGHT

They were all dressed in Kitty Lyons's creations. And they all looked fabulous!

It was Friday night, an hour before the glittering launch party for Kitty Lyons's US fashion line. For the first time all week, the 14C girls' spirits couldn't have been more excited. They all felt as if they'd been instantly catapulted into the supermodel lifestyle, as if the world was their oyster.

Even Chloe, who wouldn't be enjoying the evening with Liam as planned, was feeling somewhat pumped. It was hard not to, looking as glamorous as she did with her hair swept into a messy updo; her lips a pale, glossy pink; and her slim body poured into a strapless, flowy leopard-print dress.

Lindsay was rockin' the snakeskin mini, which she'd paired with a form-fitting white tank and white sky-high platforms.

Alexis had chosen a halter sundress in a shimmery blue batik pattern with chunky tribal-inspired jewelry.

Shiva-Rose, ever the practical one, went with the Kitty Lyons version of the little black dress — short, straight, spaghetti-strapped — which was accented with a wide tiger-print belt. She'd added matching flats and a sequined clutch.

After swapping lip glosses and blushes and taking at least a zillion giggly snapshots with their cell phones, the girls made their way downstairs. Parked outside the building a party bus was waiting to take them to Bungalow 8, which had been rented out specifically for the event. Victoria, Dan'yel, Anabelle, and Mack would already be there, in their dual capacities of partygoers-slash-chaperones, awaiting the girls' arrivals.

As the girls boarded the enormous nightclub-on-wheels, the driver stopped Lindsay. "Ms. Robinson," he said in a formal tone. "Ms. Devachan asked me to give this to you and to have you read it aloud to the girls once we're on our way."

Lindsay took the envelope he held out to her. When everyone was seated, and the bus pulled out into the traffic, Lindsay opened the envelope.

"Listen up, everyone," she said, waving the letter to get their attention. "We've got another V-mail." She cleared her throat and read:

"Good evening, models. You are now on your way to your first official public appearance as fashion ambassadors of Top Model Prep."

"Oooh," called Erica, a brunette with cobalt-blue eyes who lived on the fifteenth floor. "We're, like, ambassadors!"

"It is imperative that you conduct yourselves accordingly," Lindsay read. "That is to say, you will behave in a professional manner at all times. You will be polite, you will be appropriate, and you will be respectful of others and of your-selves. The rules are as follows: absolutely no drinking. This is an adult gathering, and there will be alcohol available. However, as not a single TMP student is of legal drinking age, ordering or accepting alcoholic beverages is strictly forbid-den. We have arranged to have a separate bar set up for you, serving bottled water, diet soda, and a wide and exciting array of mocktails."

"What, no chocolate milk?" joked Chloe, roll-ing her eyes.

Faye sighed. "I was hoping to taste champagne," she said.

Lindsay kept reading. "Any girl discovered partaking of alcohol or any other illegal substance, even in the most minuscule quantity, will be instantaneously expelled from the program."

This announcement was met with a few gasps. Lindsay paused to let the magnitude of the statement sink in, then read on.

"While we expect you to mingle with other guests, remember, the majority of these people will be strangers to you, and it is wise to be careful. You are all very attractive young women; many of you appear to be much older than you are. Expect to be fawned over and flirted with. Boys will be boys, after all, but most of these boys are, in fact, grown men. Should you find yourself the recipient of any unwanted attention or in a situation that makes you even the slightest bit uncomfortable, please find me or one of the other instructors immediately. Having said that, I also understand that girls will be girls, and there is sure to be an abundance of handsome men in attendance tonight. We insist that you maintain your dignity at all times. There is to be no public display of affection, no lewd dancing, and especially no leaving the party with anyone other than one of the TMP instructors. Barring an individual emergency, we will all depart together, as a group, at exactly midnight."

A chorus of groans rose up around the party bus.

"Midnight?"

"That's so early!"

"So much for this being the city that never sleeps!"

"Those are the rules, folks," said Lindsay, folding the letter back into its envelope. "I don't make 'em, I just read 'em."

The party bus pulled up to the club and the girls rushed to the windows to gape at the crowds gathered on both sides of the velvet ropes.

"Is that Kate Hudson?"

"Look, there's Zac Efron and Vanessa Hudgens. I love her dress."

"I see Heidi Klum. Man, I would *kill* for her legs!"

"Hey, who's that really old guy over there?"

"That's Mick Jagger."

"Oh, my God, my mother *loves* him."

"My *grandmother* loves him!"

When the driver opened the door, the girls nearly stampeded down the steps to the sidewalk. So much for maintaining their dignity. Ava (who'd been having difficulty teetering on sky-high-heeled satin Jimmy Choos in the first place, and was now craning her neck to make eye contact with Dane Cook and not watching where she was going in the second place) missed the bottom step.

"W-w-wooaahhh. . . !"

Alexis, Chloe, Lindsay, and Shiva-Rose whirled to see Ava, feathered hemline fluttering, polished gel-tip nails clawing the air for something to grab on to and screaming at the top of her lungs. They watched in amused horror as she toppled out of the bus, landing with a gloriously humiliating face-plant onto the sidewalk of Twenty-seventh Street.

Jana, who was coming down the steps behind Ava, didn't seem to notice; she merely stepped over her suitemate, who was sprawled like a heap of glittering haute-couture laundry on the cement. "Look, there's Queen Latifah. Queen . . . hi!"

In the gutter, Ava let out a pitiful little groan.

"Geez," said Chloe. "Is she breathing?"

"More important," said Alexis, "did she break a nail?"

"Nice X Games impression, Ava," Lindsay joked. "What do you do for the longboard competition?"

Shiva-Rose rushed over to help Ava to her feet. Ava looked a little dazed (but then Ava *always* looked a little dazed). Thankfully, she was more or less still in one piece. She brushed out her feathers, fluffed her hair, and smiled at the girls.

"That was kinda funny, huh?" she said. "Like, at least I know how to make an entrance." She thanked Shiva-Rose, then wobbled off on her stilettos, waving and calling out to Queen Latifah, with whom she presumably wished to discuss the importance of good comic timing.

The 14C girls were the last TMP students to enter Bungalow 8. By some unspoken agreement, they were going to do this together. They did not walk in single file with someone symbolically taking the lead, but marched forward, four abreast, shoulder to shoulder, slender curved hip to slender curved hip. And what a statement that made — like soldiers of fashion mustering their ranks, they exuded a united force of power, confidence, and glamour, while at the same time, each girl wore her unique beauty like a medal of honor, wielded it like a weapon.

And . . .

Heads . . .

Did . . .

Turn.

Cameras flashed and whispers rippled through the crowd.

"Who *are* they? They're gorgeous. They're *fabulous*."

Inside the club, the lights were soft, the music was loud, the outfits were outrageous, and the people were important. As expected, the biggest names in fashion were there: the biggest-name designers, photographers, models, and their agents. But there were also movie stars (and their agents) and rock stars (and their agents) and pro-sports heroes (and their agents). At a party like this, Alexis understood, an agent was a must-have accessory, like a Kate Spade purse. Unless of course the agent was of the superpowerful variety, like Eileen Ford, who was more the equivalent of a Birken bag. Maybe if Alexis schmoozed well enough, she'd be able to secure an agent for herself tonight.

Their entrance mission successfully accomplished, the girls gracefully parted company.

Alexis spotted Dan'yel across the room and practically glided over to him. Without preamble, he introduced her to the people he was with.

"This auburn-haired little imp is our beloved Alexis," he said. "Our little bundle of dynamite."

Alexis shook hands with the two elegant women and one lanky man in coke-bottle glasses; he was geeky-hip, good looking with a fashionably nerdy edge. Alexis figured he either invented the Pentium processor or the gladiator sandal.

"Alexis was our Challenge One winner," Dan'yel gushed, "which is huge! Huge!"

Alexis affected a modest smile, and the hipster geek forced himself to congratulate her while the women sipped their appletinis and acted as if they couldn't care less about Challenge One.

Hmm. Well that didn't go quite the way Alexis would have liked. Maybe Shane was right about getting used to rejection.

Glumly, she excused herself and made her way over to where Kitty Lyons, the guest of honor, stood surrounded by admirers, among them

Victoria, Mack, and Shiva-Rose. The other people hovering around Kitty were pure glamazons, both male and female, and one reed-thin girl, a particularly Bohemian-looking sort, wearing shredded blue jeans and a shrunken-tee bearing the PETA logo. Alexis wasn't really an expert on do-gooder organizations, but she did know that the PETA folks were all about the animal rights.

Alexis recognized immediately that Kitty had come by her feline-inspired nickname honestly. She was petite, with pale green eyes and sandy-colored hair highlighted with thick apricot streaks. All you had to do was add whiskers and a tail, and maybe toss her a ball of yarn to play with. Her personal style was surprisingly understated. Kitty's designs were outrageously hip and very funky, but the outfit she wore tonight was simple and pretty: a fitted, bateau-neck dress, sleeveless, made of butter-colored silk shantung, with a demure, mid-thigh hemline. Her shoes were a slightly darker yellow, mules with (you guessed it) kitten heels. Alexis couldn't help being a little disappointed. She'd expected to find Kitty in something flashy, like head-to-toe zebra print, or perhaps a leather bustier. Well, Alexis supposed, if Vera Wang were here, she probably wouldn't be wearing a tulle-and-satin wedding gown.

Lindsay skittered over and joined the circle just as Alexis arrived. In true egomaniac mode, she didn't bother to wait for an introduction from Victoria.

"I totally *love* the snakeskin," she said, posing to showcase the way her backside filled out the miniskirt. "It's so earthy, so primitive. So *real*."

One of the admirers laughed, practically snorting her drink through her nose. Another looked Lindsay up and down and snickered. "She's kidding right?"

Alexis could see that Victoria was mortified; the headmistress shot Lindsay a warning look, but Lindsay was oblivious. Mack and Shiva-Rose exchanged worried glances.

"Why would I kid?" asked Lindsay. "I really do love snakeskin. And those crocodile cowboy boots you sent over to TMP—I would have worn them myself but they weren't my size. I'm just crazy about genuine croc skin. Belts, purses, sandals. Can't get enough of it. Heck, just send me to the Everglades with a shotgun and I'll be one happy girl."

Victoria was trying desperately to get Lindsay to stop talking, pursing her lips and miming a key-turning gesture in front of them, the universal sign for "shut up!"

To her credit, Kitty did not laugh, or snicker, or slap Lindsay across the face, which, as far as Alexis could tell, was exactly what the chick in the PETA shirt wanted to do. "You're mistaken, darling," she said in a tone that was part patience, part pity. "Those boots are mock-croc. And that skirt you're wearing — it's faux snakeskin, or as I like to call it, fakeskin."

"Fake?" Before Lindsay could stop herself she wrinkled her nose and said, "Ewwww."

Victoria dropped her head in shame and let out a groan.

"Eww?" mimicked the PETA chick.

Lindsay was a runaway train. "Hey!" she snapped, all up in the activist's face. "I did *not* put in twelve-hour workdays on the set of *Yes, We Blend* to wear fakeskin. Or pleather! No! I did it so I could afford to buy things like crocodile pumps. Wearing genuine snakeskin is a right."

"It is." PETA-chick's eyes flashed. "If you're the *snake*!"

"Relax," said Kitty, calmly placing a gentle hand on the animal crusader's shoulder. "She's young. This is part of the mission. To enlighten, to educate." Kitty turned to Lindsay. "So what you're saying is that you are physically repelled by the thought of wearing man-made synthetic materials, but sporting skin that's been shed by a reptile who slithers in the dirt is your idea of glamorous?"

Lindsay deflated. "Well, when you put it that way . . ."

Alexis would have liked to stick around and see just how Lindsay Loudmouth would get herself out of this one, but a sudden storm of camera flashes near the entrance announced that someone wonderful was arriving.

And that wonderful someone was Shane!

As Lindsay struggled to dig her way out of the politically incorrect hole she'd dug for herself, Shiva-Rose felt a gentle nudge from Mack. Discreetly, they separated from the group and found their way to the dance floor.

"You look incredible," Mack told her as — being careful to maintain a respectable space between them — they began to sway to the music. "That tiger-print belt is hot."

"Faux tiger," Shiva-Rose corrected, grinning. She looked around at the shimmering club and its shimmering inhabitants. "I honestly can't believe I'm here."

"Believe it," said Mack, putting his hands on the small of her back and pulling her ever so slightly closer. "You belong here, Shiva-Rose. You're one of these people."

Shiva-Rose's glossed lips turned down slightly. "Not really. I mean, okay, so Kitty Lyons is civilized enough not to slaughter living creatures in pursuit of the perfect purse, but that doesn't make her the Dalai Lama. The majority of these people are utterly vapid."

Mack laughed. "Present company included?"

Shiva-Rose blushed. "You know what I mean."

"I know you just made a broad, not to mention insulting, generalization about the fashion industry." Subtly, he pulled her closer to him. "I'm doing a photo shoot for *Vanity Fair* next week," he whispered. "It was supposed to be last Thursday, but we had to reschedule because the model happens to be an oncology intern at New York-Presbyterian Hospital, and she was assigned to the pediatric cancer ward that day." Mack gave her a condescending smile. "Now does that sound vapid to you?"

Despite his pompous attitude, Shiva-Rose couldn't help but feel sheepish. "You're right. I was stereotyping."

Mack smiled in a more understanding way. "It's all right. Just do me a favor and don't tell Victoria I've got this *Vanity Fair* gig, okay? Technically, I'm under contract with TMP, and I'm not supposed to be doing outside jobs."

A tiny knot formed in Shiva-Rose's stomach. He was lying to Victoria . . . again. She didn't want to be part of his deceit, but she didn't want to rat him out, either.

"Sure," she said halfheartedly.

"That's a good girl."

The patronizing tone in his voice made Shiva-Rose bristle. She stopped dancing abruptly. "I'm going to get a drink," she said, and strode off the dance floor.

"I can sneak you a real one," Mack offered, following her.

Shiva-Rose kept walking. "No thanks," she said curtly. "Frankly, I'd rather die of thirst."

That stopped Mack Scarborough dead in his tracks.

• • •

Alexis threw her arms around Shane. He looked as if someone had just torn him off the cover of *GQ* in his crisp, white dress shirt, unstructured black blazer, and narrow indigo jeans.

"Hey, beautiful," he said, giving her a squeeze.

"I didn't know you were going to be here," said Alexis.

Shane laughed. "Neither did I. Graham called me about an hour ago and invited me. His manager set it up."

"Remind me to thank his manager," Alexis said, smiling up at Shane. "Where is Graham anyway?"

Shane pointed to the bar, where Graham was talking to some major league baseball player who was famous for pitching no-hitters and cheating on his wife.

Graham waved them over.

"Do you mind if we go over there?" Shane asked, his eyes shining. "I'm a huge baseball fan, and that guy is, like, my hero. I've got his rookie card in a frame on my bedroom wall back home."

He sounded like a little boy, which Alexis found irresistible. "Sure, let's go. But I'm not allowed to drink any alcohol. TMP rules. To be honest I probably wouldn't, even if they said we could."

"No problem," said Shane. "I respect that."

They wove their way through the crowd to where Graham was lounging against the bar. He introduced them to the baseball star, and Shane immediately blurted out the story of the time he hit a home run with the bases loaded to win the championship game.

"Was that in the minors?" the pitcher asked.

"Uh, no."

"College ball?"

Shane shook his head. "Little League, actually. But it was one of the greatest moments of my life."

The pitcher laughed. "I feel ya, pal. I still remember my first perfect game. I was eight years old, and the only reason we won was because the other team's starting lineup was out with the chicken pox."

Shane leaned down toward Alexis. "Know what I consider another of the greatest moments in my life?" he whispered in a voice like cream. "Meeting you."

Alexis's heart leaped at the sweetness of his words. She was in danger of melting.

Just then, a beautiful brunette in a very short dress ambled by, and the pitcher left to follow her.

"Dude," Graham said to Shane, "this party rocks."

"That it does," said Shane, slipping his arm around Alexis's waist like it was something he'd been doing his entire life.

"Woah. Man. Who is *that*?"

Alexis followed Graham's gaze across the club and saw the "who" in question.

Chloe.

She was standing at the center of a group of older women, all of whom were aging fabulously (or, thanks to modern medical science, not aging at all). These women were fashionistas of the highest order, the modeling world's revered ones, peers and contemporaries of Chloe's mother. Chloe was smiling and nodding politely, but Alexis would have bet her entire Barneys booty that Chloe wanted nothing more than to escape.

No doubt the dowager supermodels were regaling poor Chloe with stories of the times they'd worked with Charlotte, anecdotes about posing for Francesco Scavullo in the morning, lunching with Helen Gurley Brown in the afternoon, then partying long into the night at Studio 54 and living to tell the tale.

Surely they were comparing Chloe's ethereal beauty to Charlotte's, admiring Chloe's cheekbones (better than her mother's), evaluating her eyebrows (not quite as perfect as her mother's), and raving over her pouty lips (exactly like her mother's).

Alexis grinned at Graham. "That's Chloe," she said. "My roommate."

"Shut *up*! You, like, *know* her? You, like, *live* with her?"

"I, like, *do*."

"Oh, man!" Graham put his hands on Alexis's shoulders and looked her straight in the eyes imploringly. "Dude, you *gotta* introduce me."

"Sure," said Alexis. "C'mon."

When Chloe spotted Alexis approaching, she looked grateful enough to weep.

"Excuse me, Chloe," said Alexis, "but Mack asked me to find you. He needs us all on the dance floor, something about a photo for next year's TMP summer program brochure."

"Oh, thanks, Alexis." Chloe turned a disappointed look to her mother's friends. "I hate to go, but you know how it is. A model's work is never done."

"Isn't that the truth," said one of the ex-models, smiling. At least, Alexis thought she was smiling; hard to tell what with the amount of Botox that had been injected into her face.

Another of the older models had slipped into cougar mode and was eyeing Shane hungrily. "And who are you with, darling?" she asked, reaching out to touch the toned triangle of chest exposed by his half-unbuttoned shirt.

"Uh . . ." he nodded to Alexis. "I'm with her."

Alexis thought she heard the model mutter something that sounded like, "Not for long, not if I can help it."

"No, doll," purred another member of the cougar pack. "She means who are you *with*, as in what agency?"

"Oh. I'm signed with Product."

The cougars seemed to approve. Alexis was ready to get out of there. So was Chloe.

"Nice seeing you all," said Chloe. "I'll tell my mom you said hi." With a dainty wave, she led Shane, Graham, and Alexis to a relatively quiet corner of the club.

"Chloe," said Alexis, "this is Shane. And *this* is Graham."

"Hi, Shane," said Chloe, then turned her sparkling blue eyes to Graham. "Hi, Graham."

Graham had a goofy grin on his face. "Nice to meet you, Dude."

Chloe shot a quizzical look at Alexis.

"He calls everybody Dude," Alexis whispered. "Just go with it."

"Okay." Chloe turned back to Graham, who said:

"Dude . . ."

"Yes?"

"Did it hurt?"

Chloe blinked in confusion. "Did what hurt?"

"Did it hurt when you fell from heaven? 'Cause, Dude, you are, like, an *angel*."

Shane rolled his eyes, and Alexis giggled.

And Chloe (although it was one of the oldest and stupidest come-on lines in the book) found herself completely and utterly charmed.

"As a matter of fact, it didn't hurt at all." She looked up at him with sultry eyes and bit her lower lip flirtatiously. "But I have a question for you, Graham."

"Dude, go for it."

"Are those astronaut pants you're wearing? Because your butt is out of this world."

It took Graham a moment to get it, but when he did, he gave Chloe a dazzlingly lopsided grin. "Wanna dance?"

"Absolutely."

The angel and the astronaut hit the dance floor.

Lindsay had recovered commendably from her awkward moment with Kitty Lyons. She made a genuine apology (a skill that was virtually foreign to her) and then listened to Kitty and the PETA chick explain their views on animal rights. After hearing what they had to say, Lindsay was sincerely contrite. Seriously, how would she feel if some fashion-forward tigress were traipsing around the Serengeti sporting a pair (well, actually, two pairs) of strappy sandals made out of genuine Lindsay Robinson skin? She'd be peeved. Definitely.

Now Lindsay was dancing with Ava and two members of an about-to-be-huge new boy band. Mack (whom she'd noticed getting almost cuddly with Shiva-Rose earlier) was snapping pictures of the four of them, so Lindsay made sure to smile just so and not respond to the boys too obviously. The better looking of the two band members was hitting on her in a major way, and kept trying to put his hands on her hips, but Lindsay deftly avoided his moves. Not that she would have minded dancing close with him, but it was against the rules and she was sure Victoria would have a heart attack.

"Hey," called Alexis, pushing her way through the crush of dancers with her buff boy toy in tow. "I love this song!"

"Me too," said Lindsay, the energy of the moment warming her to her roommate.

Still dancing, Lindsay introduced the boy band member (Jack? Zack? Zeke? Really, did it matter?) to Alexis, who introduced Shane. They had to shout to be heard above the music.

"Where's Chloe?" Lindsay asked.

"With Shane's friend, Graham, over there."

Alexis pointed, and Lindsay turned to see Chloe dancing with a gorgeous blond guy with high cheekbones, who also had what might well have been the cutest butt Lindsay had ever seen. *What about Liam?* Lindsay wondered.

"And look," Alexis chirped. "Shiva-Rose found herself a new hottie! I bet Mack is totally jealous!"

Lindsay glanced away from Chloe to see Shiva-Rose coming onto the floor. Her dance partner was cute, too, the quintessential "skater-boy" from the top of his skully hat to the tips of his Vans. *Well, good for us,* Lindsay thought, twirling a little closer to band-boy and finally letting him rest his hand on her waist. *The 14C girls are owning this place.* She threw her head back and laughed; it was a great look, a perfect pose. She hoped Mack would catch it on camera, but she knew there was little chance of that happening now that Shiva-Rose was on the dance floor; his lens was directed only at her. And he didn't seem too thrilled about seeing her with that Ryan Sheckler wannabe.

Band-boy was attempting to get up close and personal with her again. Lindsay studied his full, pouty lips, wondering what it would be like to kiss him. Should she or shouldn't she? They were sufficiently hidden by the crowd so that Victoria wouldn't see, but still. . . . All she needed after the Kitty Lyons fiasco was to get busted for kissing the next Joe Jonas. She glanced around at her suitemates to see how closely they were following the rules.

Well, you could have driven a Porsche Cayenne through the space between Shiva-Rose and her partner. And Shane and Alexis were keeping it pretty PG as well. And Chloe . . .

Hmm. Strange.

Chloe had stopped dancing entirely.

She was standing perfectly still, like a deer caught in the headlights of the aforementioned Porsche. And on her pretty face was the same terrified expression the proverbial deer would be wearing as the speeding high-end SUV barreled toward it.

Lindsay turned to see what Chloe was gaping at.

And suddenly, she was gaping, too. But not in terror.

In amazement.

Chloe was gaping at a guy who'd just walked in the door of Bungalow 8. And Lindsay couldn't blame her.

Because the guy was full-on dazzling.

The guy was tall, tan, and tempting.

The guy was the very embodiment of the sun-soaked California beach hottie. She instantly recognized him from the pictures she'd seen on Chloe's iPhone.

The guy was Liam Lattimore.

No good deed goes unpunished.

Chloe stood there on the dance floor, not moving, and the words of the old adage screamed in her head. No good deed goes unpunished. And here was the proof.

How had she been so stupid?

She had been about to send the all-important text message to Liam after acting class. But Alexis had interrupted her. And Chloe had put aside her own concerns to help Alexis the klepto.

(That was the good deed.)

And Chloe had been so distracted by Alexis's issues that she'd forgotten to hit the SEND button.

She had never pressed the SEND button! Never sent the text telling Liam *not* to come to New York.

And now he was here.

(That was the punishment!)

(Sort of.)

"Dude? You okay?"

Chloe was vaguely aware that Graham — who she'd found totally enticing seconds before — was speaking to her, but she couldn't bring herself to reply. All she could do was stare at Liam, *her* Liam, entering the club and looking around — for her, of course. He'd flown across an entire country just to see her and here she was with Graham.

Well, wouldn't that just make her the biggest hypocrite on earth? Hadn't she just freaked out over Liam hanging with Juliet Rivers?

Chloe felt sick to her stomach. Sick, and sad, and confused.

"Chloe? Dude, what's wrong?"

"I'm fine," she managed at last. "Um, Graham . . . I've gotta go. I'm sorry."

She turned and fled the dance floor. Just left him standing there.

And she didn't look back.

Lindsay was fast. She disentangled herself from the boy-band singer and made it to the entrance before Chloe was even ambulatory.

"You must be Liam."

He stopped scanning the crowd and turned to Lindsay, surprised, but clearly pleased, to be recognized. "Yeah. Do I know you?"

She shrugged one shoulder in a modest gesture. "You do if you ever watched *Yes, We Blend*."

Recognition registered on his face. The corners of his mouth quirked upward and Lindsay suddenly felt a little weak in the knees.

"Right. You're . . . Linda Robbins?"

"Close. Lindsay Robinson."

"Yeah." Liam grinned. "You're friends with Jules."

"Heard you two were pretty cozy out there on the coast."

Liam didn't confirm or deny, simply stuffed his hands in the pockets of his khakis and smiled again.

Good smile. Darn good smile. Again, Lindsay felt herself go wobbly. The pictures in Chloe's iPhone (and the shots she'd seen of him in *Us Weekly*) didn't do him justice. In photos, he was obviously good-looking but seemed sort of generic and dim. In person he exuded charm, and came off as so much more than just another cutie.

He was dressed exactly as you'd expect the son of a conservative senator to be dressed: quality navy blue blazer over a periwinkle oxford-cloth, button-down shirt, a Brooks Brothers tie loosened slightly (only slightly) at the collar, easy-fitting khakis, and Sperry shoes with no socks. Perhaps he wanted to be prepared, should he suddenly get the notion to swing up to Connecticut and enroll at Choate. It was a camera-ready, "smile-and-say-'Republican'" outfit, no doubt selected for him by his father's political handlers.

The thing was, though, he looked *good*. Because under all that prep was a body sleek with surf muscles and an attitude that exuded relaxed California confidence.

The boy smelled like sunshine.

He was eyeing Lindsay's snug miniskirt, and Lindsay did not have a problem with that at all. She shifted her weight slightly, imperceptibly, but enough to make the mini work for her.

"So, Lindsay . . ." he gave her a lazy smile. "How many anacondas had to die for that skirt?"

"None, actually. It's rain forest approved."

He laughed. "Nice."

"Ya think?"

Before Liam could reply, Chloe appeared and flung herself into his arms. Well, Lindsay noted irritably, not 'flung' exactly. Chloe was not the type to fling herself at anyone. What she did was 'waft.' She *wafted* into Liam's arms. Like a sweet-scented white mist.

Good move. Darn good move.

"I missed you so much," she said, her slender arms around his neck, her big blue eyes locked on his.

"I missed you, too, sweetie."

"How long can you stay?"

Liam didn't answer. Instead, he bent his head and gave Chloe a long, lingering kiss. A clear violation of the No Public Display of Affection rule cited in the V-mail. But Chloe didn't seem to care. Her arms tightened around his neck; his hands went to her waist.

Lindsay averted her eyes, frowning. Where was Victoria — Chief of the Kissing Police, Special Agent for the Purity Squad — anyway? Shouldn't she be busting in right about now, shouting. "Freeze, dirtbag!" or "Step *away* from the model!" or something like that?

But Victoria the Make-Out Cop didn't show, and the kiss grew more intense.

Disgusted (or maybe just plain jealous — but she wasn't going to go there yet), Lindsay stormed away.

It was true what they said: There's never a cop — or a headmistress — around when you need one.

CHAPTER NINE
BOY TROUBLE

"Victoria?"

Victoria, sipping a pink drink, turned to Lindsay. "Yes?"

"I was wondering . . ."

Victoria suddenly raised her glass to Lindsay as though toasting her. "Excellent damage control in the Kitty Lyons situation, by the way."

"Thanks." Lindsay fluttered her lashes and affected the wide-eyed innocent look she'd perfected back in her sitcom days. "So, I wanted to ask you. Didn't you say PDA was against the rules tonight?"

"Yes, I did." Victoria was instantly on alert, setting down her drink and glancing around the packed club. "Why? Is one of the girls behaving inappropriately?"

"Not that *I'm* aware of," said Lindsay, but she glanced purposefully in the vicinity of where Liam and Chloe were still sucking face.

Victoria gasped and set off at a near trot toward the couple, pink liquid splashing out of her glass as she went.

Lindsay could only imagine what Victoria would say when she reached them: "Chloe Huntley, remove yourself from that boy's lips *immediately*!" or, "Wait until your mother hears about this," or even, "Wow, that stay-on lipstick really does last through anything. . . ."

Didn't matter what she said, Lindsay decided. As long as Chloe was busted.

On the dance floor, Shiva-Rose noticed that Alexis and Shane seemed to be having a difficult time keeping their hands off each other. At least for them, she thought enviably, the temptation was mutual. Shiva-Rose was not feeling a similar attraction to her skater-boy, who kept attempting to make full body contact. She was doing an admirable job of fending him off, but frankly, it was getting old. He was cute, but she'd agreed to dance with him only to avoid talking any more with Mack.

At that very moment, Mack himself was glaring at them from the periphery of the dance floor.

Shiva-Rose hated that his obvious jealousy flattered her. Hated that even while she was dancing with another boy, her thoughts were on the photographer. He'd been such a patronizing jerk earlier. And he was a liar.

But he was handsome, and so talented. He made magic with a camera; he saw things ordinary people didn't. She couldn't help but admire that. And they had an undeniable chemistry.

She wished she didn't like him. But she did.

A few feet away, the 14A girls were dancing in a circle around a hunky, hotshot young rapper who was dripping with diamond pendants. Surprisingly, the six tons of jewelry he was sporting didn't inhibit his ability to bust some amazing hip-hop moves. And Faye, to Shiva-Rose's surprise, was doing a great job of keeping up with him — in fact, the born-and-bred New York City girl seemed to be teaching the rap star a thing or two. Maybe he'd put her in his next music video!

Then the thumping techno music was fading into a ballad. Faye and the rap star began to slow dance. Faye's roommates looked at each other glumly.

Skater-boy reached for Shiva-Rose, but she sidestepped him.

"I think I'm gonna sit this one out," she said as sweetly as she could manage.

The skateboarder looked crestfallen.

"I'm sorry."

"C'mon, please."

Shiva-Rose sighed. Not only were his puppy dog eyes making her feel guilty, but now Mack was approaching them. If Shiva-Rose didn't dance with the skateboarder right now, Mack would surely ask her to dance with him, and after the way he'd acted earlier she did not want to give him the satisfaction. She was about to tell the skater she'd changed her mind when he suddenly stumbled forward as though he'd been shoved from behind. Hard.

"Yo!"

Skater-boy whirled around, his jaw set. "What's up with that?" he demanded of the rap star, who was the closest to him and therefore the most likely perpetrator.

"What?" the rapper asked.

"You pushed me."

"I didn't push you." The rap star let go of Faye and gave the skater a challenging look.

Skater-boy pushed up the sleeves of his Billabong hoodie and stood tall. "I think you did."

But it hadn't been the rap star who'd shoved Skater-boy.

And Shiva-Rose knew it.

Victoria cleared her throat.

Liam went right on kissing Chloe.

Victoria cleared her throat again, more loudly this time. Through the open doors of the club she could see a throng of paparazzi on the sidewalk. Unfortunately, the paparazzi could see Chloe and Liam, still lip-locked.

"It's the senator's kid and the Huntley girl!" one of the photogs shouted.

"*Us Weekly*'ll pay a bundle for these shots. Hey, Lattimore, can you move in a little closer. . . ."

Victoria gasped loudly, clasped Chloe by her shoulders, and yanked her away from Liam.

"You of all people should know better," the headmistress hissed in Chloe's ear.

It took Chloe a moment to drift back to earth.

Liam's kiss had sent her head spinning. The familiar feeling of his hands in her hair had made her delirious.

But Aunt Vickie was right. Chloe did know better. A camera flashed, and the burst of light was like an accusation, snapping her back to reality. "Oh, no!" she gasped, covering her face with her hands. Liam stepped quickly away from the entrance and farther into the club, turning his back to the photographers. Luckily one of the bouncers had the presence of mind to close the doors.

Vickie was just about to read Chloe the riot act when a scream from the dance floor caused them all to turn and look.

It was Faye who had screamed. Skater-boy and the rap star were throwing punches. The skateboarder aimed a left hook at the rapper's jaw, but the rapper ducked and the skater's fist narrowly missed connecting with Faye. She shrieked and staggered backward, slamming into a waiter who was carrying a tray of drinks. The glasses crashed to the floor, shattering everywhere. Like magic, four enormous bouncers appeared on the dance floor and dragged the combatants apart, then out of the club.

For a moment, everyone just stood there in silence, not knowing what to say, or where to look. Finally, the DJ made a stupid crack about it not being a party until something got broken, and resumed the music. After an awkward moment, people began to dance and mingle again.

Shiva-Rose, trembling, stood on the edge of the dance floor. She watched as the 14A girls led a visibly shaken Faye to the ladies' room. Faye's arm was bleeding where a piece of a broken martini glass had cut her, and Shiva-Rose felt her heart contract at the sight. She glanced around to see if anyone else was hurt. Fortunately, Alexis and Shane had been dancing at the far end of the dance floor when the fight broke out and both were unscathed. Lindsay and Chloe seemed fine as well. As for Shiva-Rose, Mack had materialized at her elbow just as the fight erupted and pulled her out of the crowd to safety.

Shiva-Rose was glad to be unhurt, but there was no way she was going to thank Mack for saving her.

Because she'd seen what happened. And she would confront him about it later. She knew how it would go down: She'd tell him what she saw, and he would say it had been an accident, nothing more. He'd say he'd been making his way through the crowd and he'd simply bumped into the skateboarder.

But he'd be lying.

Mack had been the one to shove Skater-boy.

And he'd done it on purpose.

Needless to say the midnight curfew was changed to an immediate departure time. Dan'yel and Anabelle rounded up the girls and wrangled them out the back door to avoid the photographers in front. Victoria did a head count, said in a no-nonsense voice, "Nobody move," then marched back inside, probably to apologize to Kitty Lyons for leaving early. Dan'yel and Anabelle followed her. Mack was around the corner, haggling with the livery company and trying to track down their party bus. It was only ten thirty, and the driver had originally been told to return at twelve.

Lindsay sighed and leaned against the graffiti-covered brick wall of the alleyway. Surveying her twenty-nine competitors, who all looked shaken, she decided their first official outing as TMP fashion ambassadors had not gone well at all.

Covertly, she watched Chloe, who was also standing apart from the group of models. Evidently, Chloe had gotten over the embarrassment of being scolded by Aunt Vickie. She looked happy now, her famous pale blue eyes shining with a dreamy glaze that Lindsay understood was the direct result of a long (albeit public) make-out session with the boy of her dreams.

What did that feel like? Lindsay wondered. Having a boy to dream about and, better, knowing he was dreaming of you right back? In spite of the distance between them and all the drama with Juliet Rivers, Chloe had slipped right back into Liam's arms as if she belonged there.

Is that what it meant to have history with someone? To have been with them day in and day out through stupid things like chemistry class and not-so-stupid things like the Homecoming dance and Winter Formal? To recognize his voice on the phone, to know his middle name, his favorite band, how he takes his latte? Lindsay guessed it was.

She'd grown up on a soundstage where time was money, so you worked as long as you could, leaving almost no time for making friends outside of work. She hadn't gone to a real school; the studio provided an on-set tutor for its child actors. By the time Lindsay had started high school, she'd felt alien and out of place, not accustomed to taking normal classes and dealing with the pace of a school day.

And as far as her castmates were concerned (Juliet included), there was always unspoken competition among them—they'd bicker over who had more lines in a given episode, they'd rub it in one another's faces when one got nominated for a Nickelodeon Kids' Choice Award and another didn't. They even fought over salaries (well, their mothers and managers—often their "momagers"—did, at any rate). Lindsay knew all TV productions didn't operate like that, but *Yes, We Blend* had been a pretty cold place. Honestly, the only thing she missed about it was the fame. Well, that and craft services.

And as far as boyfriends went, there just hadn't been the opportunity. She didn't get to meet many boys her age, and the ones she did meet seemed interested in her only because she was famous. Not exactly the stuff true love is made of.

So Lindsay Robinson had never had a real boyfriend. Never been in love.

And she hated that the realization of that made her feel just the tiniest bit choked up.

Lindsay was so lost in her thoughts she almost didn't hear her cell phone ringing. She fished it out of her Kitty Lyons faux-fur bag and checked the readout. It was an LA number. Weird. Who could it be? She had Juliet's number plugged into her cell phone. Was it an agent? A producer? Somebody about to give Lindsay Robinson her old life back?

Her heart pounded.

She opened the phone, and spoke with confidence and aplomb.

"Lindsay here."

"What's up?" asked a male voice. A very appealing male voice. She felt a small shiver of recognition. It couldn't be . . . could it?

"Who is this?" she demanded.

"Liam Lattimore," came the breezy reply.

Lindsay flushed all over. She'd been right! What was he doing calling her? Why wasn't he calling Chloe? She cleared her throat and asked bluntly, "How did you get my number?"

"My dad's a senator. I had him run it through the CIA."

Lindsay's eyebrows shot upward. "Seriously?"

"No." Liam laughed. "I called Juliet and got it from her."

Cute *and* resourceful.

Lindsay cast a glance at Chloe. "Where *are* you?"

"I'm still in the club."

There was a long, awkward pause. Again, Lindsay glanced at Chloe, who was still looking dreamily content.

"What do you want, exactly?" she asked. She assumed he'd want her to go over to Chloe and deliver some message. Which was ridiculous — why couldn't the boy have called up his girlfriend himself?

"I want to see you."

That . . . she hadn't been expecting.

Uh. Okay.

She forced herself to sound cool, indifferent. "When?"

"Tomorrow afternoon. For, like, coffee or something."

Or something sounded good to Lindsay.

She was surprised but not shocked. So she hadn't imagined the connection, the spark, between her and Liam.

Then again, she hadn't imagined his kiss with Chloe, either.

She wondered what Chloe would do if she knew that right this very minute the love of her life was asking out a girl he'd just met who happened to be standing less than twenty feet away from her.

She'd have an absolute meltdown, that's what she'd do. It would be ugly, *and* it would linger, not unlike a bad spray tan, which would basically guarantee that Chloe would fail the commercial audition challenge.

Hmmm. Can you say, "America's Next *Flop* Model?"

And then a strange thing happened. Lindsay heard herself say, "No, thanks."

"No?" On the other end of the phone Liam sounded baffled.

Heck, Lindsay was pretty baffled herself. But she'd said it, and now she had to stick to it.

"Don't take it personally, Liam," she said coolly. "It's just that you've got an awful lot of baggage at the moment. I mean, you may or may not be hooking up with my ex-castmate, and you may or may not be in love with my roommate. Love triangles are hard enough, but a love rhombus? I'm so not going there. So . . . see ya." Smiling, she snapped her phone closed.

Lindsay was sure her former on-set tutor would be delighted to know that after all these years she remembered what a rhombus was, and that she had even been able to use it in a sentence. A sentence in which she basically dissed the gorgeous heir-apparent of one of America's most powerful political families.

Not to mention the boyfriend of her biggest rival.

The party bus was pulling up now, which was fine with Lindsay, because (a) she was way over-dressed for hanging around in a side street in Chelsea, and (b) she really didn't want to dwell too long on *why* she'd dissed the gorgeous Republi-kid.

Because she had a feeling that the answer just might include words like *nice* and *decent* and *fair*.

And who needed that?

CHAPTER TEN
DEEP DISH

Alexis was in big trouble.

Well, what else is new? she thought, padding into the shadowy common room in her slippers and pajamas. It was nearly one in the morning and she couldn't sleep. She had something on her mind, and that, coupled with the excitement of the party and the fight and the quick exit, had her all pumped up.

"You can't sleep, either?" came a voice from the sofa.

Alexis flipped on the light and saw Chloe sitting on the sofa. She was wearing a giant Crossroads Academy jersey (probably Liam's), plaid cotton pajama bottoms with electric-green chenille socks. *Yeesh*, thought Alexis, *this girl looks better in her PJs than most girls look in their prom gowns.*

Alexis shook her head. "It's adrenaline," she said.

"It's starvation," said Shiva-Rose, appearing in the doorway, tugging on her bathrobe. "I barely ate anything at that party. My stomach is growling."

"And your mouth is babbling," Lindsay called from the darkened room behind Shiva-Rose. "Shut up already. I'm trying to sleep."

"Maybe the girls across the hall are still up," Chloe suggested. "They have the best snacks in the whole dorm."

"Yeah, maybe we can mooch some Doritos from them," said Alexis, feeling her stomach growl, too.

The three of them headed for the door.

"Did I just hear someone say Doritos?" Lindsay bolted into the common room. Alexis bit back a laugh.

They crossed the hall quietly and knocked on the door to 14A. It opened quickly and there was Jana, wearing a black silk nightie and holding a canister of sour cream and onion flavored Pringles.

"Welcome to insomnia central," she said.

On the sofa, Faye held up a bag of Fritos. "Also known as the pig-out zone."

Ava, who had just stuffed half a devil dog into her mouth, just waved.

The 14C girls entered and dove happily into the junk food.

"I'm so glad Victoria is not into the waif look," said Alexis, grabbing a handful of peanut M&Ms.

"So what did you think of the fight?" Ava asked, wiping chocolate crumbs from her chin. "The skater guy thought the rapper pushed him, but I don't know . . ."

"He didn't push anybody!" said Faye, licking orange Cheetos dust from her fingers.

"That's 'cause he was too busy being all over *you*!" Jana teased her roommate, and Faye just smiled.

Alexis glanced at Shiva-Rose, who said nothing. Alexis had an inkling about what had gone down, but she didn't want to bring it up now.

They talked about Kitty Lyons and how cool she was, and about the food and the music and the bouncers, who were roughly the size of grizzly bears on the outside, but (according to Ava, who'd spent a good part of the evening flirting with them) were more like teddy bears on the inside.

"That guy you were with was amazing," Jana said to Alexis. "Are you guys, like, an item or something?"

Alexis was surprised to find herself blushing as she thought of Shane, how sweet and attentive he'd been all night. "Yeah, I guess we are."

"His friend—the 'Dude' dude—he was way cute, too," said Faye. She'd directed that comment to Chloe, who pretended not to hear. "I introduced him to Victoria and he even called *her* Dude."

"He can call *me* anything he wants," said Ava. "And any *time* he wants."

Alexis noticed that Lindsay was being weirdly quiet. She also noticed that Lindsay's phone vibrated several times, but for some reason she wasn't bothering to answer it.

"You and Liam," said Jana, nudging Chloe, "are so incredibly cute together."

It was Chloe's turn to blush. "Thanks," she said. "It was *so* good to see him."

"You guys were, like, totally into that kiss," said Ava.

"And the paparazzi were totally into you guys being totally into it," Alexis observed, feeling a pang of jealousy that no one was snapping pictures of her and Shane. "I bet it's, like, all over the Internet tomorrow."

"I'm cool with that," Chloe said sweetly.

Again, Lindsay stayed silent.

Then Ava launched into a story about a boy back home, and how he'd tried to kiss her in the hallway at school, but she'd been so nervous she dropped her history book on his foot and broke his pinky toe.

Finally, the junk food was gone, and at twenty minutes to four, the stuffed, sleepy 14C girls went back to their own apartment.

On the bunk below Alexis, Shiva-Rose fell asleep almost instantly and across the room, in her single bed, Lindsay was curled up with her face to the wall. Alexis was aware of Lindsay tossing and turning for a while, but she finally dozed off, too.

Alexis didn't even bother to try to close her eyes, and when the first hazy rays of a New York sunrise glowed softly against the window, she slid down from the top bunk and went into the common area where, grinning like a dope, she spoke the thought that had kept her awake all night, the words that had filled her heart with a kind of shimmering joyful energy that had made it impossible for her to sleep.

"I am in love with Shane Cooper," she whispered into the silence.

Shane, the NYU student, the packer of picnics, the sweeter-than-sweet guy who still got excited about his Little League victory, was not the kind of guy who would fall for a girl from Alexis's background, a girl who stole things, who had no proper upbringing and a brother in juvie.

Yep. She was in big trouble all right.

Or was she? No one had ever looked at her the way Shane did, and he *had* said that meeting her was one of the greatest moments in his life. Maybe he was the kind of guy who could overlook her past, and help her create a fabulous future.

She honestly didn't know. But that didn't change the fact that she was in love with him. And that was going to be trouble.

With a heavy sigh, Alexis dropped herself onto the sofa.

She immediately sprung up again, because she'd sat on someone's cell phone: Lindsay's. The touch screen had lit up, and there was no way Alexis could avoid seeing what it said.

Lindsay had six new text messages and eight missed calls.

And every single one of them was from Liam Lattimore.

Apparently, Alexis wasn't the only resident of 14C who was headed for trouble.

Alexis sat on a bench and watched the NYU summer students enjoy the warm Saturday. She had never in her life considered going to college — she barely showed up for high school — but suddenly, it seemed like something she should put on her list.

If she won the TMP contest and got a modeling contract, she'd be able to afford the tuition. And although her grades at Hamtramck were only okay, she wasn't stupid. She'd get in somewhere, she was certain.

Definitely worth looking into.

Her cell phone rang, and when she checked the caller ID her stomach flipped over. It was the number of the pay phone at the juvenile detention facility, the phone her brother was only allowed to use for five minutes, twice a month.

Alexis was afraid to answer, but she was more afraid not to.

"Hey, Nick."

"I got the stuff," he said in that growl of his that made Alexis shudder. "Looks expensive."

"That's because it is."

"Yeah? I traded one of them girly colored shirts for a carton of cigarettes."

Alexis rolled her eyes. The cigarette dealer certainly got the better end of that deal. Those pastel Lacoste polos had cost close to a hundred bucks apiece. But all she said was, "That's great."

"Send more stuff. Soon."

Not a suggestion, not a request. An order.

Alexis's heart gave a sick thud. "I don't know if I can . . ."

He cut her off. "Soon, Alexis. I'm not screwin' around, either."

She reminded herself that, for the moment at least, Nick was behind bars and he couldn't hurt her. But she still heard herself say, "I'll try."

Thousands of miles away in Detroit, Nick gave a wicked-sounding chuckle and hung up. Alexis tucked her phone into the pocket of her jeans and took a long, steadying breath.

"There's my girl," came a cheerful voice. Shane was approaching her with a dazzling smile.

Alexis hopped up from the bench, the awful phone call vanishing from her mind. "I have a great idea," she practically sang. "Let's go shopping."

CHAPTER ELEVEN
POETIC JUSTICE

At ten thirty, Chloe opened her eyes and smiled. The sun was streaming in through the curtains in her private room, and she felt suffused with joy and peace.

Liam was in New York.

She would be able to spend the whole day with him, sightseeing like silly tourists — walking over the Brooklyn Bridge, going to see the Statue of Liberty, kissing at the top of the Empire State Building. Or maybe just hanging out in his suite at the Hudson Hotel.

Either plan worked for her. She was just so happy that things had been sorted out between them, just so happy that he'd come all this way to see her.

Just so happy.

Except for two things.

She rolled over onto her back and stared at the ceiling.

One "thing" was her mom, who would no doubt find out that Liam had shown up against her wishes.

And the other was . . . Graham.

The boy-unlike-any-other that she'd met last night.

Graham had been funny and out-there and just plain bold. Hanging out with him had felt strangely liberating.

She didn't know what he did or where he went after she'd so rudely left him standing on the dance floor last night. Everything had gone crazy, between Victoria catching her with Liam, the paparazzi, and the quasi-celebrity boxing match on the dance floor. Maybe Graham had just left the party right after Chloe ditched him, and went home alone to nurse his broken heart. Then again, maybe he'd found another girl to dance with and he had had the time of his life, forgetting about Chloe entirely.

That second option shouldn't have bothered her, but it did, a little.

She rolled out of bed, wandered into the bathroom, and took a long hot shower. She knew Liam wouldn't be dragging himself out of bed until well after noon, so there was no reason to rush. She dressed casually in denim cutoffs, a Free People peasant blouse, and ballet flats, then sent a text for Liam to read when he woke up.

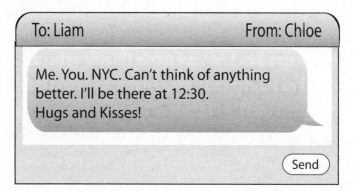

To: Liam   From: Chloe

Me. You. NYC. Can't think of anything better. I'll be there at 12:30. Hugs and Kisses!

Send

On her way through the common room, she saw that the door to the other bedroom was ajar. The sound of deep measured breathing told her that at least one of her roommates was still asleep. She hoped it was Alexis. The idea of Alexis out alone in the city made Chloe nervous. It was a shoplifter's wonderland, after all.

Whatever. She didn't want to worry about that now.

She grabbed a notebook and headed for the roof.

Secrets fill the space between us
And promises,
    like petals pulled from daisies,
        scatter in the wind
Forgiveness is not trust

Still, I close my eyes and fall into the warmth
Accepting, but not believing

And waiting, always waiting
    For the one thing . . .
        you cannot seem to give

Chloe scribbled out the fourth line, then changed "waiting" to "longing." Then she tore the page from the notebook, crumpled it into a ball, and stuffed it in her shorts pocket.

"Yuck."

Usually, Liam left her feeling inspired. But she wasn't feeling that last poem. At all.

It was eleven, and the late morning sun was scorching here on the roof. But the New York skyline glittered, and a manic music — sirens, car horns, bus brakes — rose into the air like a soundtrack, loud but oddly comforting to Chloe.

She put pen to paper again and wrote:

He calls me angel
But he is the one with heaven in his eyes

God that's corny, Chloe thought, grinning down at the words. But she didn't cross them out. Instead, she gave the poem-in-progress a simple title: "Graham."

Weird how in the first poem, which was for Liam, she used pronouns like "us" and "you." But when she was writing about Graham (something she hadn't intended to do at all) she called him "he." Well, he was a virtual stranger, that's why. There was still distance between them. Composing verse *about* him was one thing; writing a poem *to* him seemed just a little too intimate, for the moment at least.

But why was she even writing a poem about another boy when the love of her life was only several city blocks away at this very moment?

"Am I interrupting something?"

Chloe looked up to see Shiva-Rose stepping through the door and out to the rooftop. Her roommate — she must have been the one asleep in the other room — wore terry cloth short-shorts, a tank, and flip-flops. She looked a little wan, as if she hadn't slept well, and her dark eyes were full of emotion.

"No," Chloe replied. "It's fine. I was just . . . never mind."

Shiva-Rose's eyes flickered to the notebook. "Were you writing something?"

Chloe shrugged.

Shiva-Rose clearly decided not to push it.

"What about you?" Chloe asked. "What are you doing up here?"

"Well . . ." Shiva-Rose hesitated, biting her lower lip. Then she seemed to decide to finally open up. "I came up here to . . . pray, actually."

To Chloe's credit, she didn't scoff or giggle. She noticed that Shiva-Rose was holding a small white book in her hands.

"To say Kaddish, actually," Shiva-Rose went on, her voice soft. "It's the Jewish prayer for the dead." She swallowed hard and continued. "My mother died. A year ago today."

Chloe felt a wave of raw emotion crash over her. She hadn't been prepared for that confession.

"I'm so — so sorry," she stammered. "I didn't know . . ."

No wonder, Chloe thought. No wonder Shiva-Rose had always seemed so closed off, so protective of herself. She studied her roommate with new eyes.

Shiva-Rose sat down next to Chloe, and for a moment the two of them sat in the relative silence of the rooftop. Then Shiva-Rose spoke again, her voice trembling only a little.

"She was a preschool teacher. She was amazing at it, too. She had unbelievable energy, but she also had incredible patience. And she loved to sing and tell stories." Shiva-Rose looked out over the rooftops, but her eyes were far away, remembering.

"I bet the little kids loved her," said Chloe.

"They did. And she loved them, too." Shiva-Rose sighed and her lower lip quivered slightly. "There was this one little boy . . . Oren. He was such a little character, always smiling, laughing. Well, anyway, his family was really poor, like so poor, they couldn't even afford school supplies. And he would always have to borrow everyone else's crayons. My mom said it broke her heart, especially because no matter how many times he had to ask to borrow the crayons he never once forgot to say please and thank you to the other kids."

Absently, Chloe's fingers went to the embroidery along the hem of her blouse; she remembered paying $127 for it and thinking it had been a steal. She wondered how many crayons could be bought with $127.

"Well, my mom decided she was going to buy a box for him. So one day after school, she went into town to the little stationery store and bought him a giant, brand-new box of crayons. And on her way out of the store . . ."

Chloe wasn't sure when the tears had started to stream down Shiva-Rose's face. She wasn't sure when her own had begun, either, but they had, because she knew where this story was leading.

"On her way out of the store," said Shiva-Rose, "there was this explosion . . . not a huge one but big enough. It was a suicide bomber . . . and my mother was thrown twenty feet into the air. . . ."

Chloe put an arm on Shiva-Rose's shoulder.

"A witness said all he remembered seeing were these intense flames and then hundreds of brightly colored crayons, raining down from the sky and landing on the sidewalk."

"I'm so sorry," Chloe said again, her tears flowing freely now. "Shiva-Rose . . . I am so very, very sorry."

"I miss her."

The words cut into Chloe as she thought of her own mother. She felt guilt and anger and heartache all at once. She wasn't the world's greatest daughter, but her mother just made it so difficult for the two of them to be close. It was always about Chloe not living up to Charlotte's dreams and expectations. But what about Chloe's dreams? Didn't Charlotte know how precious it was to just have each other, to just love each other?

Chloe made a silent promise to herself to try to make things better with her mother.

"Would you like to have a little time alone?" Chloe offered.

Shiva-Rose sniffled and nodded. "Thanks."

Chloe gathered her pen and her notebook and headed for the stairwell. She felt herself trembling, just a little bit, as she thought about Shiva-Rose and what she'd been through. Her own problems seemed so trite by comparison.

She tried to focus on the day ahead of her, how wonderful it would be to spend the afternoon with Liam.

But in her mind a new poem was beginning to reveal itself.

A poem about love.

And flames.

And crayons.

Chapter Twelve
Lindsay's List

REASONS TO GO OUT WITH LIAM LATTIMORE

1. HE'S GORGEOUS
2. HE'S RICH
3. HE'S GORGEOUS
4. HE CAN TEACH ME TO SURF
5. SENATOR'S SON = MAJOR PUBLICITY

Sitting cross-legged on her bed, Lindsay read the list and underlined the second *gorgeous* three times. Then she wrote:

REASONS *NOT* TO GO OUT WITH LIAM LATTIMORE

1. Chloe

She let out a rush of breath and rubbed her forehead. Being nice and fair and decent was giving her a migraine.

At that very moment, Lindsay knew, Chloe was off with Liam. Lindsay had seen her roommate prance out of the apartment looking fresh faced and eager to see her boy. Lindsay hadn't said a word to her about the fact that Liam had been in touch with her.

Liam had sent Lindsay a bunch of text messages last night, asking her to meet him for coffee. She'd ignored them all.

She wasn't a complete idiot. She knew Liam wasn't looking to make some deep, lasting love connection with her. He was probably only reacting to the fact that she was forbidden. And that she'd turned him down. She well knew the golden rule: *Boys always want what they can't have.*

And if she did break down and sneak off to go out with him, then what? Best case scenario they'd date secretly for a month, two tops, and then he'd move forward. Or, more likely, backward—to Chloe.

Wouldn't *that* be a kick in the head?

Lindsay tucked the pen into her notebook and tossed it to the foot of the bed, which sent the pen flying. It rolled across the floor and under Alexis's dresser.

But what if she *did* decide to take the risk and go out with Liam?

Something had definitely ignited when she met him. She'd tried not to acknowledge it, but in those few minutes she'd spoken to him (before Chloe and her turbo-charged lips had entered the picture), they'd made a connection. She smiled now, remembering his crack about anacondas dying. His humor was a lot like hers. They *got* each other.

And there was no way to deny the physical attraction. The *mutual* physical attraction.

Ignoring his text messages had not been easy. She had a feeling they could talk for hours about everything, about nothing, and he'd laugh at her wisecracks and she'd laugh at his.

Lindsay's phone vibrated. It was Liam. *Quelle surprise.*

Deciding to put an end to this once and for all, she answered.

"Hi, Liam."

"Finally! Does this mean you're going to meet me later?"

"Nope." Something occurred to Lindsay. "Wait, aren't you with Chloe *right now*?"

"Yeah, we're having a late lunch at Butter. I told her I had to go to the men's room."

Well, that explained all the flushing noises in the background.

"So your plan is to finish your date with Chloe, then go out with me? In the same afternoon?"

"What can I say? Call me an overachiever."

"Oh, there are a lot of things I'd like to call you, Liam, but 'overachiever' isn't one of them."

Liam laughed. "You've got a quick mind, Lindsay. And you're funny. That's what I like about you."

Lindsay was no relationship expert, but she assumed that calling a girl and asking her out while you were on a date with another girl broke about nine zillion dating rules.

Lindsay was shocked that even someone as entitled as Liam would have the nerve to try it. And that he was trying it on *her* made her angry. Did she *look* like a girl who would tolerate being the "other woman"? No.

But the problem was that in addition to feeling shocked and angry, Lindsay also felt a little bit flattered.

Flattered that even when he was on a date with the gorgeous Chloe Huntley, he was still thinking about her. Somewhere deep down she was afraid that made her pathetic, the antifeminist. But she couldn't help how she felt.

"You don't like me, Liam. You don't even know me."

"Well I *want* to know you. So what's it gonna take?"

"A miracle."

He laughed again. "C'mon. Gimme a break, will you? I'm making a major effort here. I mean, I'm hiding in a public restroom, just to talk you."

He had a point. Lindsay grinned in spite of herself. "Most guys just send roses."

"You like roses?"

Lindsay sighed. "Of course I like roses. Pink ones. But that's irrelevant. The thing is, Chloe is my . . ." she almost said *friend,* but that wouldn't have been remotely accurate. "Chloe is my roommate." Then Lindsay forced out the next words, knowing them to be all too true. "Going out with you would just be *wrong.*"

Liam was quiet for a moment. "I'm not giving up, you know."

"Well, good luck with that," said Lindsay. "Now get out of the men's room and go back to your date.

Oh, and don't forget to wash your hands. Bye."

She hung up and flopped backward in her bed.

He wasn't giving up.

That's what he'd said: *He wasn't giving up.*

The thing was, Lindsay couldn't decide whether that completely ticked her off . . . or made her the happiest girl in New York.

CHAPTER THIRTEEN
OVER

Shiva-Rose, still drained from her experience on the rooftop, entered the classroom building. It was Saturday, so she knew no one would be around. Which was why she asked Mack to meet her here.

He was waiting for her in the photo studio. He looked as dashing as he always did, but for the first time since meeting him, Shiva-Rose wasn't thrown off-kilter by his good looks or charm. She knew what she had to do.

Before she could say a word, though, he handed her a fat oversize envelope.

"What's this?" she asked.

He was grinning like crazy. "Those are the pictures from the ferry ride."

"Oh." Shiva-Rose had come here on a very specific mission, and she didn't want to be side-tracked. "Listen, Mack . . ."

"Don't you want to look at them?"

Shiva-Rose shrugged.

"Well, you can do that later, I guess. But the really good news is that I sold them."

So much for not getting sidetracked. "You sold them? To whom?"

"A new Italian fashion magazine. This guy I know, he used to be an editor at *Vogue* over there in Milan, he's starting up his own magazine. He's calling it *Dolce Vita,* and it's going to blow all the other magazines out of the water. And guess who's going to be featured in the first issue? I already got the check. Five thousand euros, and half of it is yours."

Shiva-Rose gasped. For one thrilling moment, she was overcome. *Me?* she thought in awe. *Featured in a glamorous international magazine? And getting paid for a real modeling job?* What would her friends back home say? Rahm? Her dad? It was a dream come true!

But then reality came crashing back on her. The reality of her being enrolled at Top Model Prep.

And of what Mack had done. Against her wishes.

"Mack, you can't do that!" she exclaimed.

He titled his head to one side, and she couldn't tell if he was confused or angry. "What do you mean I can't do that? I did it. End of story."

"I told you it was against the rules. I told you to withdraw the photos!" Furious, she flung the envelope onto the floor. "Look, I may not have any experience in this business, and I'm definitely no lawyer, but I do know enough to know that you can't sell pictures of me without a legal agreement or a contract. And did you forget that I'm a minor? I'm sure you've got to have some kind of parental consent."

"Well, with anyone else, I would have done the paperwork." Mack folded his arms across his chest and his jaw flexed. "But since it was you . . . since it was us . . . I figured we could do it on a handshake."

"That's just it, Mack," said Shiva-Rose. "There *is* no us."

Some of the bluster went out of him when he heard that. "I thought . . ."

"I know what you thought, and for a while there, I was thinking it, too. But last night"—she paused to take a deep breath, dragging her hand through her hair—"last night I saw a side of you I really didn't like. You didn't want me to slow dance with that boy so you pushed him. You started a fight."

Mack's eyes darted sideways, but he didn't deny the allegation.

"People could have gotten seriously hurt!" Shiva-Rose cried. "Faye was cut and bleeding! And you didn't even own up to any of it." It felt almost good, unleashing all her anger on him. It had also felt good to cry up on the roof, to tell her story to Chloe. Maybe today was all about Shiva-Rose finally letting go. "And another thing," she added, her dark eyes flashing, "all this lying makes me really uncomfortable. I don't want to be involved with someone I can't trust."

A crackling silence filled the studio.

Finally, Mack bent down and snatched the envelope off the floor. "Fine. You had your chance. And if you tell Victoria about any of this . . ."

He trailed off. He didn't have a ready threat, and Shiva-Rose knew it. In this situation, *she* held all the cards. He knew it, too.

"I believe those are mine," Shiva-Rose said coolly. She stretched out her hand.

He hesitated only a moment before handing the envelope to her.

"Cancel the deal with *Dolce Vita*," she said. "Or I'll tell Victoria everything."

With that, Shiva-Rose turned and strode out of the studio, envelope in hand.

"Most girls would kill for an opportunity like this," he shouted after her.

Shiva-Rose kept walking. He was right, of course. But she wasn't most girls. If she was going to be a success in this or any business, she was going to do it the right way. Without cheating.

Would she ever have another chance to be featured in an Italian magazine? She had no way of knowing. But there was one thing she did know for certain:

Her mother would be proud of her.

And that was worth more than all the euros in the world.

CHAPTER FOURTEEN
THE TRUTH

On Sunday morning, Alexis announced to her roommates that she was taking them to SoHo House for a day of luxury pampering. Use of the club's upscale spa had been part of her winnings from Challenge One, and she wanted to share it with them.

"I'm in," said Lindsay, who'd been jonesing for a full-body seaweed wrap for over a month.

"Me, too," chimed Shiva-Rose. A massage and a facial were just what she needed after the drama-heavy weekend she'd endured.

"I invited Shane and Graham to meet us for mocktails on the roof afterward," she said. "Hope that's okay with you guys."

No one had any objections to that. Least of all Chloe, although she forced herself not to show it. "I'm seeing Liam off at the airport," she said. "But I'll meet you guys at SoHo House as soon as I can."

"Cool," said Alexis.

Then Chloe went downstairs to grab a cab to JFK, and Shiva-Rose excused herself to go across the hall to return a bottle of nail polish remover she'd borrowed from Jana.

When Alexis and Lindsay were alone in the common room, Lindsay cut right to the chase.

"You did it again, didn't you?"

Alexis blinked. "Did what?"

Lindsay rolled her eyes. "Forget it, Alexis," she said calmly. "I found the sweaters you stole. And no, I wasn't going through your stuff. I dropped a pen yesterday, it rolled under the bureau, and when I bent down to get it, I saw two sweaters stuffed behind the dresser. So, either you're the world's biggest slob, or you shoplifted again and didn't want us to know about it."

For a moment the two girls just stared at each other. Alexis, feeling like a cornered animal, went on the defensive. "So what if I did? Are you gonna go running to Victoria and tell her the piece in the tabloid was true? Or maybe this time you can just call Barbara Walters and she can announce it on *The View*. But, before you do, you might want to consider that I'm not the only one with a secret here."

Lindsay lowered one eyebrow quizzically. "Meaning . . . ?"

"You've got something going on with Liam. I saw the text messages, so don't even bother trying to deny it. So go ahead and rat me out to Victoria, but if you do, I'm going to tell Chloe that you're hitting on her boyfriend. Then she'll go crying to Aunt Vickie, who'll find an excuse to throw you out."

Lindsay's eyes burned into Alexis's. "For your information, Alexis, I wasn't going to rat you out."

"You weren't? 'Cause that definitely seems like something you would do."

"Yeah, well, apparently I'm turning over a new leaf," muttered Lindsay, shaking her head. "What I was going to say is that you need to do something about this problem. Like see a shrink."

"That's what Chloe said."

Lindsay narrowed her eyes. "That would be Chloe whose boyfriend I'm scamming on, right?" The words dripped with sarcasm.

Alexis sighed heavily. "I'm sorry. I was just . . ."

"How did you know about those texts anyway? Did you go through my messages?" The irony of that possibility wasn't lost on Lindsay; she had started all of Chloe's Liam troubles by going through Chloe's phone. Talk about karma.

"No, not exactly." Then Alexis proceeded to explain about sitting on Lindsay's phone. She was surprised when Lindsay laughed.

"I'm pretty sure you're telling the truth," said Lindsay. "'Cause nobody could make that up."

Lindsay hesitated a moment, then decided to go for broke. "And as long as we're telling the truth, I should probably mention that I was the one who leaked your shoplifting adventure to the press."

"Yeah, I figured it was you." Alexis's eyes narrowed. "Nobody else is that sneaky. You really would do anything to win, wouldn't you?"

"I would have, at first," said Lindsay. "But like I said, I'm trying to work through that." She laughed. Alexis didn't. "Okay, I know it was heinous. I shouldn't have done it."

"Are you gonna do it again?" Alexis asked.

Lindsay shook her head. "I told you, I'm trying to make a change for the better. And anyway, sabotage is exhausting."

Alexis smiled warily. "All right. I'll take your word for it. If you'll believe me when I say I'm gonna try to stop shoplifting."

Lindsay considered quoting Yoda: "Do. There is no try." But she decided to let it rest for the moment.

"What are you going to do about Liam?"

"Nothing." Lindsay told Alexis all about Liam calling her from the men's room and his promise not to give up. "I'm hoping he'll just get bored and go away."

Shiva-Rose returned then, and after some quick preparations the girls headed out for the SoHo House.

In the cab on the way uptown, Alexis thought about the sweaters she'd stolen. She'd had to be extra careful since she was with Shane at the time, but she'd pulled it off. Before, that would have made her proud. Now, it just made her sick to her stomach.

Lindsay spent the cab ride deleting all the messages and voice mails Liam had left for her. Some small part of her would have liked to save the cute ones with the flirty compliments, but she didn't. She simply read them once, then hit ERASE.

It seemed like the wise thing to do.

CHAPTER FIFTEEN
FRIENDS

High above the Meatpacking District, on the roof of SoHo House, the girls were led to a table overlooking the street. Shane—the billboard version of him—was still chillin' in his underwear. The human version would be arriving any minute.

Chloe was feeling a little nervous about seeing Graham after the way she'd treated him. She hoped he wouldn't completely ignore her, or worse, tell her off, although he had every right.

The thing was, she'd begun to wish she hadn't blown him off for Liam. Her and Liam's romantic day sightseeing around New York hadn't gone at all as she'd hoped it would. Nothing specifically horrid had occurred, except he had disappeared for a while during lunch. He'd said he was just going to the men's room but she had her doubts, since he was gone for such a long time. On the scale of one to ten, the day had been a solid six. Well, maybe a five and a half. The problem was that the spark she'd expected to feel at being reunited with Liam just never seemed to ignite.

Then, this morning at the airport, she'd tried to read him the poem she'd written for him. Usually, she'd send him poems by text, or even handwrite them on pretty paper and give them to him to keep. Reading a poem to someone out loud, as far as Chloe was concerned, was a big deal. It meant something. But she'd mustered up the courage and before he went through the security checkpoint, she'd read the heartfelt lines she'd composed for him.

And when she was finished baring her soul to him, Liam (who'd been searching through his backpack for his boarding pass the whole time she'd been reading) had only one thing to say.

Not, *Wow, Chloe, that was beautiful.* Not, *thank you, that means a lot to me.* What Liam said was:

"There'd better be a good in-flight movie this time."

What Chloe said was, "Good-bye, Liam."

There were already four tall glasses of ice water waiting for them. As they settled into their chairs, Alexis asked, "Does everyone feel pampered and relaxed?"

"If I were any more relaxed I'd be in a coma," quipped Lindsay.

"Best mani-pedi I ever had," said Chloe truthfully.

"That masseuse was incredible," Shiva-Rose said with a lazy sigh. "She loosened up muscles I didn't even know I had."

"Speaking of muscles . . ." Lindsay motioned toward Shane and Graham, who were just arriving. Shane was wearing a tank top that showed off his biceps, triceps, and every other muscle in his extremely buff arms. Graham was wearing a button-down shirt, which he hadn't bothered to button, revealing his six-pack abs.

"I do love the dress code in this place," joked Alexis.

When the guys sat down, Chloe kept her eyes on her water. She could feel Graham keeping his eyes on her.

"How was the spa?" Shane asked, slipping his arm over the back of Alexis's chair.

"Oh, it was great, we . . ."

Chloe felt an urgency bloom inside her. Before she could question it, she popped up from her seat like a rocket. Graham immediately followed her with his eyes, and she met his gaze.

"Graham, can I talk to you for a second? Over there?"

Graham stood and followed her to the far end of the rooftop. Chloe felt her heart pounding and could hear the whispered remarks of her roommates and Shane.

"Think she's gonna push him off the edge?" Lindsay joked drily.

"Only if he doesn't jump first," said Shane. "Poor guy's been majorly depressed since she blew him off on Friday."

"Yeah, that was pretty harsh," Alexis conceded.

"But there were extenuating circumstances," Shiva-Rose said.

Lindsay sipped her water. "Extenuating circumstances named Liam."

Put Liam out of your head for now, Chloe told herself as she and Graham crossed the rooftop patio. Then they stopped and faced each other stiffly. Chloe had never really felt awkward around a boy before. Why was Graham so different?

Nearly a full minute passed before either of them spoke, and when they did, it was at the exact same moment, nervously and suddenly.

"I'm writing a poem about you . . ." Chloe blurted, feeling her face turn crimson.

Just as Graham was saying, "Dude, I wrote you this poem . . ."

They looked at each other and again spoke simultaneously:

"*You* write poetry?"

Graham smiled. Chloe laughed.

"Yes, I do," she said, feeling her tongue loosen and her spirits lift. Finally, she could share her secret passion! "I write, I read it. Anything by Maya Angelou I absolutely love, and, of course, the classic stuff by Robert Frost and William Carlos Williams." Chloe hazarded a glance at Graham, in case he was about to make fun of her.

He didn't. His eyes were shining. He was being . . . earnest.

"Dude, 'The Love Song of J. Alfred Prufrock.' By T. S. Eliot. Best poem ever."

"I've never read that one."

"You should. It's awesome."

More awkward silence. Graham slid his hands into his back pockets; Chloe examined her fingernails.

"I'm sorry about Friday," Chloe said at last. "I know what I did was totally rude. It was just that this guy showed up. . . ."

"Your boyfriend."

Chloe sighed. "Yeah."

"It's cool," said Graham, trying not to sound hurt and failing epically. "I guess I should've known a girl like you would have a boyfriend."

Chloe took that for the compliment it was. "I didn't mean to lead you on," she said, and even to her it sounded lame.

"Dude, it's fine. Really."

"So . . ." Chloe forced a smile. "We can be friends?"

"Sure." Graham nodded, rocking back and forth on the soles of his Reef flip-flops. "Friends."

"Friends. Great."

"Dude . . ."

"Yes?"

"Your boyfriend . . ."

"Yes?"

"I hope that dude knows he's the luckiest guy in the world."

The words slammed into Chloe's heart like a fiery comet, and the next thing she knew she had flung (yes, *flung!*) her arms around Graham's neck and was kissing him for all she was worth.

Across the rooftop, Shiva-Rose's eyebrows shot up. Alexis giggled. Shane almost choked on his ice water.

And Lindsay, in a deadpan tone, remarked, "Guess he's not gonna jump after all."

Slowly, reluctantly, Chloe ended the kiss, but Graham kept his arms around her, and she didn't pull away. He kissed her lightly on the top of her head and whispered in a raspy voice.

"So, Dude, when you say 'friends,' I'm thinking you mean, like, really *good* friends, huh?"

Chloe laughed and pressed her cheek against his chest. "I'm not sure what I mean," she admitted. "But the good news is, we've got all summer to figure it out."

CHAPTER SIXTEEN
IT'S A JUNGLE OUT THERE

Monday was all about hair and makeup for television commercials. Again, the girls sat in front of huge vanity mirrors outlined by bare lightbulbs. Anabelle wandered around as they sat at their makeup mirrors experimenting with foundation and blush, and she explained that the look would always depend on the product.

"The idea is to look natural," Anabelle explained. "Apply your cosmetics so that they look as if you applied none. You want to appear as though Mother Nature simply wrapped her arms around you and kissed you lightly on your brow."

"What is she talking about?" asked Alexis.

Shiva-Rose indicated the thousands of dollars worth of makeup spread out before them. "We have to make it look like none of this ever happened. That we just got out of bed with rosy lips, sculpted cheekbones, and eyelashes that are long enough to cast a shadow."

Alexis quirked an eyebrow at Chloe. "But . . . she *does* get out of bed looking like that."

Chloe smiled. "Thanks, but I can't take any credit for genetics."

The girl certainly knew how to take a compliment gracefully, thought Shiva-Rose, impressed. She was really beginning to like Chloe Huntley. She had half a mind to suggest to Victoria that Chloe be allowed to student teach a special seminar in the Art of Modesty. Some of the girls were so conceited about their looks it made Shiva-Rose want to scream. Because Chloe was right—being that beautiful wasn't a personal accomplishment, it was a genetic gift. Chloe was born gorgeous and she knew it, and instead of flaunting it, she was respectful of it. Somewhere deep down, Shiva-Rose understood that she, too, had been given that genetic blessing, and being here at TMP was making her realize that, for better or worse, society puts an extremely high value on good looks. Being gorgeous could, and would, open many doors for her. The real trick would be knowing which doors to go through and which to avoid.

She came out of her reverie to find Alexis laughing. Shiva-Rose turned to see that Chloe had swept a huge blue stripe of bright lilac eye shadow down the middle of her nose, and had outlined her lips in blue. On one cheek she'd drawn three dots with pink lipstick and on the other she'd made a big black *X* with kohl eyeliner.

"If Picasso were my makeup artist," Chloe joked.

But when Shiva-Rose caught Chloe's eye in the mirror, a serious look passed between them and suddenly she knew what Chloe's artwork symbolized. Makeup was not simply to enhance, it was to intimidate. In the modeling world, it was a weapon. It was war paint. And after their conversation on the roof, Chloe had a sense of the fact that Shiva-Rose knew more about war than anyone else in this program.

Shiva-Rose picked up a tube of mascara and quietly began to stroke the black gunk onto her lashes, wishing Chloe could hear the words she was speaking in her heart: *Thanks for putting things into perspective. Thanks for understanding.*

As far as Shiva-Rose was concerned, Chloe Huntley was not just pretty on the outside. On the inside, she was downright beautiful.

. . .

Tuesday found them taking another stab at the Bubble Head script, and the exercise yielded the same results as the previous go-round. Lindsay and Chloe dominated. Shiva-Rose, in a word, sucked. Alexis battled her accent valiantly, but didn't exactly win the war.

Dan'yel said, "The more clearly you speak, the better the audience will understand what you are saying."

Lindsay leaned over and whispered to Shiva-Rose, "Duh."

On Wednesday, they were introduced to the new photographer, which pretty much shocked everyone. Girls whispered and gasped and acted as if the mystery of Mack's disappearance was right up there with crop circles and the Loch Ness monster.

"Where did he go?" asked Jana. "Why did he leave?"

"Creative differences," Victoria replied vaguely. Which explained nothing.

Alexis, Lindsay, and Chloe turned questioning eyes toward Shiva-Rose, who gave them a tiny smile, shrugged, and said, "You know how messy those creative differences can be."

The roommates made her promise to explain later.

The new photographer, Rodney Blanchette, was a nice man in his midfifties with a shiny bald head, and a calm, pleasant voice. He'd been in the business, he told them, *forever*. He had first-hand knowledge of fashion-industry history; he remembered things from the distant past like poodle perms, Cheryl Tiegs, and film. (One of the 14A girls asked Ava if she needed someone to explain to her what film was.) The day's lesson was titled "The Great Debate: Comp Card or Head Shot?"

"A head shot," he explained, "is exactly what it sounds like, a photo that is taken from the shoulders up. These are used mainly by actors, which is what you are for the purposes of this challenge. The *comp* in comp card is short for compilation, and it includes two or three shots, showcasing a model's range of looks. A facial close-up, a full body shot, big glamour, au natural . . . whatever the model is able to transform into."

He passed around samples of each. Shiva-Rose noticed that while the comp card was in vivid color, the head shot was taken in black and white.

As though reading her mind, Rodney explained, "Casting agents now like to see head shots in color, but for years, up until very recently, head shots were always in black and white only. Any thoughts on why?"

Jana raised her hand. "Cheaper to produce?"

"Good guess," said Rodney. "And perhaps that did figure into it, but according to industry legend, the reason was that when Hollywood was young, movies and television shows were filmed in black-and-white. So casting agents needed to know how an actor would look in that medium. Even after everything turned Technicolor, the tradition of doing head shots in black-and-white continued. Personally, I like the idea. It's kind of an homage to the old days. But that's just me. I'm nostalgic."

The models found Rodney's class enlightening and fun, and although he was only a fill-in photographer, they enjoyed his old-school insights.

And on the day of the challenge at the crack of dawn, they once again piled onto a party bus and headed for the second challenge. It wasn't clear to the girls where they were heading — up north, away from Manhattan — until they spotted a sign that made Shiva-Rose gasp.

Well, it was perfectly logical, of course. The Mane Event commercial was going to be shot on location, and that location was the Bronx Zoo!

"Why do we have to go so early?" complained Ava.

"We need to be there before the zoo opens," said Jana, yawning. "So we don't have to deal with a billion screaming kids."

"Early call times are part of the business," said Lindsay, who was invigorated. When the alarm clock had gone off at five, she'd hopped out of bed with enthusiasm; Shiva-Rose had only burrowed deeper into her pillow. "And the light at sunrise is very flattering. Not as good as sunset, which is called the magic hour, but it's still pretty good."

The bus pulled into the empty parking lot of the Bronx Zoo, and the girls disembarked. The instructors had arrived in a limo just moments before. Dan'yel was overseeing the unloading of the van that had transported the video equipment as well as several wardrobe racks and hair and makeup necessities.

"We're a traveling circus," giggled Alexis.

"And here comes the ringmaster," said Shiva-Rose. She nodded toward Robert McClary.

"Maybe we'll get lucky and he'll take a meeting with a hungry polar bear," said Lindsay.

Chloe rolled her eyes. "He'll probably ask the polar bear to imagine that he had a puppy. . . ."

The girls laughed, but Shiva-Rose's was forced. She was dreading this competition. When Lindsay's alarm clock woke her, she'd briefly considered packing her bags and heading back to Israel then and there. It was going to happen anyway, once this fiasco was over with. Why delay the inevitable?

"Come along, girls," said Victoria, who had gone all out for the occasion, dressing in a khaki camp shirt and tailored shorts. A silk scarf in an olive drab camouflage pattern (Did Hermes even do camo? Apparently.) was knotted loosely around her neck, and on her feet were a pair of spanking-new hiking boots.

"Dolce and Gabbana's missionary collection?" said Alexis.

"All that's missing is the pith helmet," said Chloe. "And the tranquilizer gun."

"We're heading to the African Plains section of the zoo," said Victoria. "Now please, stay with the group. I don't want you wandering off into the Baboon Reserve."

They fell into line with the others, passing through the turnstile and into the zoo to the set. The background: the lion habitat! Evidently, the lion had a later call time than the models because for the moment, there were no big cats in sight.

A makeshift camp was set slightly apart from the shooting area. Changing areas were fashioned out of curtains, and folding chairs were arranged in rows. A table had been set up, and it held a stack of hot-off-the-presses scripts extolling the virtues of Mane Event shampoo.

When Shiva-Rose saw the contingent of advertising executives milling around, she felt her insides freeze. Being humiliated on camera was one thing, but making a complete fool of herself in front of these Madison Avenue types was another.

Around her, the zoo was coming to life with the sounds of birds squawking and animals growling and screeching in the distance. She had the distinct sense that she was about to be stampeded!

The girls snatched up copies of the script and in addition to the animal sounds, the morning air was suddenly filled with murmuring of models as they began to read and rehearse the pithy pitch.

Shiva-Rose trudged to the table where the stacks of scripts sat beside a display of several bottles of Mane Event shampoo and conditioner, along with elegantly packaged tubes and jars of hair putty, styling gel, and defrizzing products—all props to inspire them. Shiva-Rose grabbed a script, and for the heck of it, a slender, tawny-colored vial of intensive repair serum, on the chance that it would bring her luck.

She took a seat and skimmed the script: "Bring out your inner lioness with Mane Event . . .", "Take 'pride' in your hair . . .", and (Shiva-Rose's favorite) "It's a jungle out there."

She actually laughed. *This* was what the advertising geniuses had spent the last week "tweaking"?

Her eyes wandered from the script to the bottle in her hand. Maybe the sleek packaging would give her an idea about how to sell this product. It really was a beautiful presentation. The plastic container was shimmery gold, and the dark print-ing was bold and fierce-looking.

She turned the vial around and read the blurb on the back: predictably boastful stuff regarding its follicle-healing properties, directions for use, and . . .

Mane Event firmly denounces the practice of animal testing in the manufacturing of its hair care products and strictly refuses to conduct busi-ness with any supplier or distributor that employs or encourages such practices. Container made of 100% recycled materials.

Firmly denounces. Wow. These words were not your typical marketing lingo. These words indi-cated passion and commitment.

The kind of passion and commitment put forth by a certain designer Shiva-Rose knew.

She stood up, squared her shoulders, and marched to the back of the room where Dan'yel was chatting it up with the ad honchos.

"Excuse me," she said in what she hoped was a businesslike tone. "I was wondering if I could make a suggestion."

Dan'yel looked wary.

One of the execs said, "Be my guest."

"Clearly, Mane Event is very proud of its animal-friendly practices. I happen to know that Kitty Lyons, the designer, is also a staunch believer in animal rights. So, I was thinking . . . maybe the Mane Event people and the Kitty Lyons people could get together and launch a joint campaign, focusing not only on the quality and style of both brands, but on your collective commitment to your shared values. I mean, think about it. Mane Event and Kitty Lyons. The idea just screams"—she paused, smiled—"make that *'roars'* tie-in."

The ad men were looking at her with stunned expressions.

"That is the most brilliant and creative outside-the-box idea I have ever heard," said one.

"I agree," said another. "The whole feline connection . . . well, the concept practically purrs!"

The other execs laughed and congratulated Shiva-Rose.

"Young lady, there's a job for you at our firm whenever you're ready," offered the first executive.

Shiva-Rose beamed. "Well, I'll leave you gentlemen to work out the details. I have an audition to do."

She began to walk away, but Dan'yel stopped her, throwing his arms around her and giving her a hug. "Brains *and* beauty!" he proclaimed. "How did you ever come up with that?"

"To be honest," said Shiva-Rose, "I think it came out of sheer panic. I'm dreading the audition. I'm terrified of saying those lines. I guess I thought if I changed the direction of the campaign, those guys would have to go back to the drawing board and come up with a whole new commercial, and I'd get a few more days before having to embarrass myself . . . again."

Dan'yel considered this. "Tell you what," he said. "I'm going to give you an exemption from Challenge Two. You've just accomplished something extraordinary. And that business sense you've obviously got will go a long way when you become a supermodel and start lending your name to product lines. You are hereby waived from having to take part in Challenge Two."

Shiva-Rose was flooded with relief. "Dan'yel, thank you."

"Of course, you won't be eligible to win it."

"Oh, that's fine," gushed Shiva-Rose. "There was never any chance of that anyway."

"I'll clear it with Victoria. I'm sure she'll be very proud of you. Now, go sit down and watch your friends compete."

Shiva-Rose went back to her seat, glowing.

CHAPTER SEVENTEEN
BEST SHOT

The audition was to go forward as planned.

The concept for the actual commercial shoot would change entirely when the ad guys had a chance to rework the campaign based on Shiva-Rose's suggestion. Victoria was already on her cell phone, explaining the idea to Kitty, who loved it even more than the ad guys did. Meetings were arranged and the execs expected to have the new concept in place within two weeks.

For now, though, the TMP girls would use the existing audition material, which featured a girl at the zoo having a bad hair day. When she sees the regal lion and his majestic mane, she gets motivated and luckily, the passing balloon vendor happens to be peddling Mane Event shampoo as well. The girl in the commercial then washes her hair in a nearby mock-waterfall (a shot involving flamingos) and is immediately asked out on a date by the handsome chimpanzee trainer.

The hair stylists went against everything they believed in and made the girls' hair look utterly ghastly, and the wardrobe people supplied them with the sort of boring clothes a person might wear for a day at the zoo: denim shorts, boring T-shirts, slumpy sweatshirts, and the like.

The girls listened to Dan'yel explain the process.

"First, I want to note that the flamingos' appearance has been cancelled."

"I wonder why?" asked Alexis.

"Maybe their agent wanted more money," joked Lindsay, but inside, her stomach was turning nervous somersaults.

"Also, the chimpanzee trainer will not be joining us."

"He must have the same agent as the flamingos," said Shiva-Rose, who was utterly relaxed now that she, like the flamingos and the chimp wrangler, was off the hook.

"And we've cut the waterfall scene," Victoria added. "Apparently, there's a rather high algae count in man-made falls, and we don't want to risk anyone getting sick."

Lindsay suspected that the cut had less to do with microscopic organisms than with the fact that the waterfall scene (and every other part of the commercial) was just plain stupid. But the TMP instructors couldn't insult the ad men by saying so.

"We'll shoot the first part of the commercial only," explained Dan'yel, "so you'll just have to recite the slogans that appear in the script while you're still in bad-hair mode. To the best of your ability, *act* like you've been transformed by the product. And we, the panel, will just have to use our imaginations."

Despite Lindsay's earlier excitement, her nerves were beginning to get to her. So much was riding on this. And with McClary judging, she was already at a huge disadvantage. She was hit with the sudden urge to call Liam, to hear his voice, to exchange their signature sarcastic barbs. That would make her feel better.

But she couldn't do that. And not just because it was only four A.M. on the West Coast.

She glanced at Chloe, who looked as though she had a lot on her mind. The typically cool, calm, and collected Cali girl seemed nervous, too.

Now Lindsay's eyes darted to Robert McClary. He was sitting with the other judges, looking as smug as ever. She could only hope that he would be professional about this.

Then Dan'yel called out, "Cue the lion," and Lindsay had to laugh.

The girls focused their attention on the broad, grassy lion habitat. It was designed to look as though the lions were roaming free on the African flatlands, so that zoo-goers could feel as if they had been simply wandering the grassy plains and quite accidentally stumbled upon the King of the Beasts.

After a few moments, the lion appeared. The girls gasped, some in awe, some in abject terror, but there was no denying that the big cat was making a grand entrance. He prowled like a four-legged dancer, his sleek, golden coat catching the early sunlight as he shook his thick, splendid mane.

Lindsay wondered who *his* acting coach was.

"First up," said Dan'yel, "is Alexis Cournos."

Alexis, looking a little like a lion cub herself with her red-gold hair and feisty walk, made her way to the mark.

"Rolling," said Dan'yel. "And . . . action."

Alexis went through the motions of spotting the lion, admiring his hair, lamenting her own, and purchasing the shampoo from the balloon vendor. "Take pride in your mane," said Alexis, smiling at the camera. "Because it's a jungle out there!"

Not bad, thought Lindsay. *Darn.*

Chloe went next, and even having a bad hair day she looked gorgeous. Her acting was more subtle then Alexis's, more internalized and deep. Good if you're performing a Eugene O'Neill play, maybe a little affected for a shampoo commercial. But, Lindsay noted glumly, McClary seemed to be buying it.

Lindsay sighed and watched as girl after girl went up and put her own spin on the inane lines and actions.

Faye's audition was a disaster. She was in a state of panic through the entire thing. Being this close to a wild animal (even though the zookeeper was called in to assure the trembling girl that the lion could not escape his habitat) did not sit well with Faye. She stuttered and forgot the lines and even tripped over her own two feet, bumping into the balloon vendor and causing him to let go of his huge bundle of balloons.

"I'm sorry, Dan'yel," said Faye, on the verge of tears as everyone watched the colorful balloon bouquet float up and away over the borough of the Bronx.

An emergency helium tank was brought in, and everyone waited while another batch of balloons was inflated.

Lindsay was last to go.

She hit her mark, looked at the lion, and emoted. She made herself become the girl in the zoo with the unfortunate tresses, the girl who, with just a little help from a really over-priced shampoo, could have everything she ever wanted.

And after spouting the clichéd, "It's a jungle out there," she gently ran her hands through her hair and roared at the camera.

She roared!

And from his place in the man-made grasslands, the lion turned and looked at her with respect.

More important, so did Robert McClary.

While the judges met to discuss the scores, the girls were told to enjoy the zoo.

Fat chance. Everyone was in a state of heightened anxiety. Still, they broke into small groups and went off to look at the animals.

Shiva-Rose, Lindsay, Chloe, and Alexis found themselves setting out together, although no one had said they were required to stay with their roommates.

A huge crowd had gathered around the seal exhibit.

"Feeding time," said Shiva-Rose, checking the guide map she'd picked up.

The girls watched as the slick little sea creatures entertained the crowd, clapping their flippers, balancing balls on their noses, diving and splashing.

"They're cute," remarked Alexis. "High energy. They seem happy."

Lindsay let out a little snort that was almost a chuckle. "That's the trick," she said. "To try and look like you're enjoying yourself while you're performing for the crowd."

Chloe slid a sideways glance at her. "Speaking from experience?" The tone of the question was surprisingly kind.

Lindsay nodded. "You perform or you don't get your reward," she said, watching as the smallest seal accepted a slimy fish from the trainer. "You've got to be good at what you do and look as if you like doing it. I bet they do have fun, mostly, but I'm sure that just once in a while they'd like it if everyone stopped looking and just let them swim."

When feeding time was over, they moved on, stopping for ice-cream cones before making their way to the bug carousel.

"Oh, we've gotta," said Shiva-Rose. "Please." Giggling, the girls each took a seat on a life-size insect, just as the carousel began to move. The music plinked and tinkled as the ride revolved.

"If someone told me before I came to New York that one day I'd find myself sitting on a giant green grasshopper," said Chloe, "I'd never have believed them."

"There are a lot of things I wouldn't have believed I'd be doing in New York," said Alexis softly.

"What are you complaining about," said Shiva-Rose, grinning. "I'm riding in a dung beetle chariot."

"Dung beetle?" Lindsay wrinkled her nose. "That's just gross."

"Do you ever feel," asked Alexis in a thought-ful voice, "like life goes in circles and no matter how hard you try, you don't get anywhere. You just keep going around and around, making the same mistakes."

Shiva-Rose, Lindsay, and Chloe exchanged glances. No one was sure what to say, so they just stayed quiet.

As the girls left the merry-go-round, Robert McClary appeared and asked Lindsay for a moment of her time.

"We'll wait for you," said Alexis, as Lindsay followed Robert toward a picnic table.

"Sit down," he said, unsmiling.

Lindsay felt as though she might jump out of her skin. Was he going to personally deliver the news that she was out? Was he that much of a jerk? But he'd liked her audition, she knew he had.

"I want to tell you," he began, "that I'm sorry for the way I behaved over the last several years."

Lindsay's mouth dropped open in shock. She certainly hadn't seen that coming.

"I was wrong about the agent thing," he said. "I knew it then, and I know it now. You were scheduled to meet him before you ever set foot in my studio."

Lindsay blinked. "Thank you," she said.

"Of course, that does not excuse your behavior in my classroom last week. I don't care how big a star someone is; they never have the right to be disrespectful."

He was right, of course. "I'm sorry," said Lindsay. She was starting to get good at this apology thing.

"And as far as the puppy monologue goes, I want you to know that it was not an oversight on my part. I brought that to class specifically for you."

Now Lindsay frowned. "To mock me."

McClary shook his head. "Of course not. To remind you of how this all began. Lindsay, in this business, people often forget where they came from. And that is when they get themselves in trouble. You've had some bad breaks lately, but I consider you darn courageous for coming here and being willing to start over. That is why I brought the puppy monologue. It was my way of letting you know that you have what it takes to do this. You always have."

Lindsay tried to speak, but her voice caught in her throat. She managed a smile.

"That's all I have to say."

With that, Robert McClary stood and walked in the direction of the lion habitat. As Lindsay watched him go, she realized that he really was a decent person, struggling to remain decent in a business that was often far from decent. It occurred to her that in some way, this handsome, proud, and talented man was the king of a different kind of jungle.

She wiped her eyes quickly and went to join her roommates.

"Let's hit the World of Birds," she suggested.

With the help of Shiva-Rose's guide map they found the bird exhibit and went inside. Hundreds of birds welcomed them with songs, squawks, and screeches.

"Boy, are they noisy," said Lindsay.

"But beautiful," added Shiva-Rose.

They stopped to admire a Cuban Amazon parrot that was preening, showing off its stunning plumage. "Kind of like us," joked Alexis.

Chloe gently touched the glass of the bird display. "Have any of you ever read a book called *I Know Why the Caged Bird Sings*?"

"I have to read it for school next year," said Shiva-Rose. "It's an autobiography, isn't it? Some poet."

Chloe nodded. For a long moment, the girls listened to the birds' song. Each note was different, every sound unique, every warble and tweet and caw was something individual and special, and although none of these sounds were ever meant to be sung or heard in unison, somehow it seemed as though the more birds that joined in, the more beautiful the song became.

"Kinda like us," Alexis said again, but this time it didn't sound like a quip.

"It's no fun being in a cage," said Chloe.

"Freedom is the most important of all human rights." Shiva-Rose nodded, pressing her hand to the glass wall as Chloe had. "I wish everyone could understand that."

Again the girls were quiet, as they reflected on their own ideas of freedom—having it, keeping it, losing it.

Barely audible above the noise of the birds came the sound of four cell phones, ringing at the same time.

"Time go back," said Lindsay.

So they did.

The girls reported back to the African Plains to face the panel of judges, which included the creative director of the Mane Event ad campaign.

"This must be what the gladiators of ancient Rome felt like," Chloe observed. "Just before they let the tiger into the Colosseum."

"Hey," said Shiva-Rose. "That's a cool image. Maybe we can use it in the campaign. A beautiful woman vamped up like a gladiat-ress, about to fight the raging tiger. But as the tiger comes running toward her, she tosses her beautiful hair, and instead of attacking her, the tiger cuddles her as though it were a kitten."

Lindsay, Chloe, and Alexis just gaped at her, openly impressed.

"How do you do that?" Alexis wondered. "You're like the Rain Man of advertising or something."

"The girl's got a gift," Lindsay said. She was surprised at how easy it had become to be complimentary. It didn't mean she was any less hungry for the win, but maybe the old saying about catching more flies with honey was right.

And it didn't mean that she wasn't scared to death. She wanted this commercial; she knew it could be the beginning of her comeback.

Dan'yel stood, welcomed them back, and then slipped into judge mode. "I was impressed with everyone's efforts," he said. "But the commercial genre is a very specific niche and some of you simply didn't find a way to fit."

He called girls forward one by one and the panel offered their critiques.

When it was Faye's turn, she crept forward apprehensively and forced a brave smile.

"Your beauty shone on camera," Anabelle said, "but unfortunately, you just couldn't seem to master the delivery of the lines."

"I agree," said Robert. "You lacked confidence, and your speaking was often garbled."

Faye's chin trembled but she managed to hang tough while Dan'yel handed down the verdict. "We're sorry, Faye, but we've given you a D-. You're going home."

Her roommates rushed to her and offered hugs of support.

Given the choice, many of the girls might have opted to spend ten minutes in the tiger cage than here in front of the judges. Nails were being bitten, hair was being twirled and tugged, knees were knocking like bongo drums. More girls were called forward. Some were praised, others constructively criticized, and still others were given the bad news that they simply did not have what it took to make it past this challenge.

Jana and Ava both received Bs, which kept them in the competition. Only one other D- was handed down, to a girl who spoke in a heavy southern accent that was all wrong for TV. A handful of Cs were handed out, and a number of Ds.

Then Dan'yel called Alexis forward.

"You were your typically spunky self," he told her. "And ultimately your accent was not as big a problem as we'd originally feared. But you didn't capture the spirit of the product — you just weren't edgy, or dangerous enough for this project. You've earned a B-plus."

The other judges concurred, but the ad man gave her a nice compliment. "For a more cutesy campaign, you'd be my first choice, hands down."

It was down to Chloe and Lindsay now.

Dan'yel called them both before the panel and said what judges always say in the final moments of any contest: "It was really a very difficult decision because both of you were so wonderful."

In this case the statement was true.

"So . . ." said Victoria, motioning for Shiva-Rose to come forward, "we are going to leave the final choice up to the mastermind of the new campaign."

Shiva-Rose's mouth dropped open. "Me? You want me to choose?"

"Well, you are the one with the vision," said Anabelle.

Shiva-Rose thought it was awfully unfair to be put on the spot like this, especially because the last two standing were her roommates. She looked at Chloe and Lindsay, who were waiting to learn their fate.

Dan'yel leaned close to Shiva-Rose and said softly, "Think like an advertising executive." Then he winked at her.

And suddenly, Shiva-Rose understood. This was a test. Once again, the teachers were endeavoring to teach them just how demanding and cutthroat the modeling world could be. Who on earth could decide between these two girls who were both so talented?

Nobody, that's who!

Shiva-Rose smiled brightly.

"Both of them get A-pluses," she announced. "I choose both of them,"

"You mean a tie?" said Victoria. "Ties are not allowed."

"Not a tie," said Shiva-Rose. "A tie-*in*. That's what we're doing now, right? A tie-in between Kitty Lyons and Mane Event and God only knows how many animal activist groups will jump on board. So my solution is to have Lindsay, whose hair is more manelike than Chloe's, represent the hair products while Chloe, whose body is more the kind Kitty designs for than Lindsay's, represent the clothing line. But they do it together."

Victoria gave her a beaming smile and the ad exec shook his head in awe.

For the girls in 14C, Challenge Two was an epic success.

CHAPTER EIGHTEEN
SECOND BEST

The girls were back at the dorm, changing out of their audition outfits. The plan was to celebrate their triple victory by putting on bikinis and heading to Washington Square Park to catch some rays. Conventional wisdom dictated that models should avoid sun damage to their skin at all costs. Teenage-girl wisdom, on the other hand, held that one should exercise any and every opportunity to be seen in a skimpy swimsuit. That's what SPF 70 was for.

Chloe was just tugging her two-piece out of a drawer when her phone rang. She hit the touch screen to answer, and before she could say hello, her mother started in.

"Second place? You came in second place?"

Well, Chloe would say this much for Aunt Vickie. She didn't waste time in delivering bad news.

"I didn't come in second," Chloe explained. "It was a tie. So, technically I won."

"A tie is not a win," snapped Charlotte. "Winning is when everyone *else* loses!"

Chloe heard herself apologizing. "I'll try to do better."

"Yes, you will," said Charlotte. "And to make sure, I'm coming out there to keep an eye on you, to coach you if need be."

Chloe wanted to scream "Don't you dare!" But then she remembered: *Flames. Crayons.*

And instead she said, "Okay. It'll be really good to see you, Mom."

Charlotte said nothing for a long time. "Well, yes, it will be good to see you, too. I've been worried about your eyebrows. Are you maintaining that arch? You never were very good at tweezing."

"You're right," said Chloe. "When you get here, maybe you can teach me how to do it."

"Young lady, I do not appreciate your sarcasm."

"I'm not being sarcastic," said Chloe, and she wasn't. "I really am looking forward to spending some time with you." She smiled to herself. "In fact, I'll take you to this great place called Max

Brenner. Something tells me they'll make a big fuss over you there."

"Oh. Well. I suppose . . . that will be . . . nice. I'll have my secretary text you my flight information. You can expect me sometime late Sunday."

"Okay."

"Good-bye, Chloe."

"Bye, Mom. I love you."

But Charlotte had already hung up. Chloe sighed, threw a tube of sunscreen into her bag, and joined her roommates in the common room.

Alexis, coming out of the bedroom, was struggling with the strings of her bikini. She turned her back to Chloe and said, "Do you mind tying this?"

"No problem," said Chloe, reaching for the strings. "Hey, what's in the box?" She motioned to a large package on the coffee table, which was wrapped in brown shipping paper.

"Oh, I just need to send some stuff home," Alexis explained. "Do you guys mind if we stop at the post office, or a FedEx place on the way?"

"That's fine," said Shiva-Rose. "As long as we get to the park before all the cute boys leave."

"C'mon, let's go," said Lindsay. "Here, I'll carry the box, Alexis. It's practically bigger than you are."

"Uh, that's okay. . . ." Alexis lunged for the box, but she was stopped short because Chloe still had a hold of her bathing suit strings.

Lindsay had picked up the box and seen the mailing label.

It was addressed to Nick Cournos, at the detention center for juvenile defenders.

A look passed between Lindsay and Alexis. Alexis's heart pounded. It felt as if a hundred years went by before Lindsay (without taking her eyes from Alexis's) said, "So . . . did anyone remember to bring a Frisbee? Because I've heard there is no better way to meet guys in the park than by 'accidentally' clobbering them with a strategically aimed Frisbee."

"I've got one in my bag," said Chloe.

"Typical California girl," laughed Shiva-Rose. "Have you got a surfboard in there, too?"

"Nope, but I do have some tofu and Governor Arnold Schwarzenegger."

Giggling, they headed out the door.

Alexis checked the back of her suit to be sure the tie was secure.

Thanks to Chloe, there was a nice little knot in her bikini strings.

Thanks to her demanding dirtbag brother, there was a big nasty one in her stomach.

CHAPTER NINETEEN
ROSES

After a few leisurely hours of sunshine, the girls headed back to the dorm, changed clothes, then waited in the hallway to say good-bye to Faye. Lindsay was doing her best not to gloat, but she couldn't help it. She'd won. She was getting back on TV. She was happy it was Faye leaving and not her. Still, she'd make a point of looking totally bummed out on Faye's behalf.

"There are so many other girls I'd rather see leave than Faye," said Alexis.

"I know what you mean," said Lindsay, and despite her recent "nice-girl" image, her eyes darted to Chloe.

Chloe gave her a frosty look, which Lindsay returned.

"Like that bleached blond with the nasal voice, Mandy, who's always talking about herself in the third person."

"I know!" said Shiva-Rose, striking a pose and mimicking the blond. "*Mandy* needs more eye shadow; *Mandy* ate three whole carrots and feels like throwing up."

"*Mandy* is a pain in the butt," said Lindsay.

The girls laughed, but stopped abruptly when the door to 14A opened.

"She's gonna be so bummed," said Chloe.

"Just be sympathetic," Shiva-Rose advised.

"Poor Faye," said Alexis.

"I bet she'll be crying her eyes out," predicted Lindsay.

But when poor Faye burst out into the hall with her suitcase, she was giggling and smiling. Her roommates followed, cheering.

"Or . . . not," said Lindsay.

"Guess what just happened!" said Faye, who was practically jumping up and down with excitement.

"We give up," said Chloe.

"Well, after the judging, which was probably the most humiliating and painful experience of my life, I came back here and started packing my stuff. And, ya' know, I was sobbing, like, completely *bawling* and feeling like I'd never amount to anything in my whole life. . . ."

"Okay . . ." said Shiva-Rose. "Still not getting the jumping for joy thing. . . ."

"So I'm looking for my magenta strapless bra, but it turns out Bikini actually took it when *she* left, because all I could find was the top of Bikini's bikini, which is also magenta, but Bikini's bikini has silver stitching and my strapless bra just has regular stitching . . ."

"Right. So you're *packing* . . ." Lindsay prompted, wanting to get to the gist of it.

"And my cell phone rings. And it's Ice Berg."

"Ice Berg?"

"The rapper I met at the party."

Chloe looked at her funny. "His name is Ice Berg?"

"Yeah. He's Jewish. He converted."

Shiva-Rose grinned. "I like it."

"Me, too!" said Faye. "Anyway, he's talking, and I can barely hear him cuz I'm still, like, bawling, and finally I get what he's telling me. He wants me to be in his next rap video!"

"Oh, my God!" said Alexis, giving Faye a hug. "That's amazing!

"I know, right?" gushed Faye. "It's, like, one minute I'm bawlin' and the next I'm . . . *BALLIN'!*"

Chloe laughed. "I think you just summed up the whole modeling business in a nutshell."

Everyone congratulated Faye and wished her luck.

"Thanks," said Faye. "Well, I've got to go. My parents are coming in to meet with Ice Berg's manager and sign all the paperwork. I'll let you all know when the video airs! Oooh, I'm gonna miss you guys!"

"We'll miss you, too," said Chloe as Faye practically skipped down the hall.

"Mazel tov!" Shiva-Rose called after her.

"Wow," said Lindsay as the girls went back to 14C. "That's a big break." She made a mental note to look into auditioning for music videos herself. She could totally hold her own with Beyoncé, but she'd never be able to pull off a Taylor Swift. Country was not Lindsay's thing.

"Speaking of big breaks," said Alexis, entering the common room. "You and Chloe definitely got yours today! You each booked a national network commercial!"

Chloe perched on the arm of the sofa. "Thanks to a certain advertising prodigy," she said, smiling at Shiva-Rose, who was flopping into a chair.

"Don't thank me," said Shiva-Rose. "You guys totally earned it. You were great."

"I have a question," said Lindsay. "I understand the whole tie-in thing, the crossover campaign concept. But does that mean . . . well, I'm just wondering . . . will there be separate commercials, like, one for the hair stuff and one for the clothes, or . . ."

Chloe rolled her eyes. "What she wants to know is, are she and I going to have to work together? Are we going to be forced to appear in the same commercial at the same time?" She fixed Lindsay with a disgusted look. "Apparently, as far as Lindsay is concerned, the entire television-viewing universe isn't big enough for the both of us."

"Is that what you were getting at?" Alexis asked Lindsay.

Lindsay felt a little embarrassed. "Kinda. I mean, c'mon. I know you guys think I'm a total mean girl, but let's be honest. Chloe and I don't exactly have professional chemistry. And, if I'm going to be completely truthful, when it comes to certain things—okay, most things—I just don't like to share."

At that moment, there was a knock at the door. Alexis answered it to find a deliveryman.

"Is dis faw-teen C?" he said in a heavy New York accent.

"Yes."

"I got a deliv-uh-ry fo' you." He turned and called down the hall. "Okay, guys. Dis is duh place. Bring 'em in."

Alexis hopped away from the door as another deliveryman, and another, and still *another* marched into the common room, each carrying an enormous, perfect bouquet of long-stemmed roses!

"Is this a joke?" asked Lindsay.

"If it is," said the deliveryman, "it's an expensive one."

When the parade of deliverymen finally ended, there were twelve dozen fragrant rose bouquets decorating apartment 14C.

"Hope you girls got a lotta vases," the deliveryman said, handing Alexis a clipboard to sign.

"Is there a card?" she asked.

The man handed her a tiny rectangular envelope. "Give 'em plenny a' sunlight. Fresh wadda ever two days. And watch out fuh the thawns."

"Thawns?" said Alexis.

"Yeah, thawns. Ya' know. Dem pointy tings on duh stems."

"Oh. Thorns."

"Dat's what I said. Watch out fuh dem thawns. Dey pinch like a sonuvagun."

"Right. Thanks."

Alexis closed the door and for a moment, the models simply stared in shock at the new state of their common room.

"Geez," said Alexis. "I hope none of us are allergic."

Shiva-Rose touched one of the delicate blossoms. "It looks like a florist shop in here."

"Or a funeral home," said Lindsay.

Chloe was smiling and her eyes practically glistened as she took it all in. "A dozen dozen roses," she said. "It's the most romantic thing ever."

"A dozen dozen," repeated Lindsay. "How many roses is that. Like, a hundred and forty?"

"A hundred and forty-four," corrected Shiva-Rose.

"Oh." Lindsay guessed her former on-set tutor would be disappointed, but she didn't care. "Dat's a lotta flow-uhz," she said, mimicking the deliveryman.

Alexis was looking at the little envelope in her hand. "It's not addressed to anyone," she said. "The front of the envelope is blank."

"Read the card," said Chloe.

Alexis opened the envelope, slipped the card out, and read.

She hesitated, then read it aloud. "It says, 'I'll be back in two weeks. Love . . . Liam.'"

Chloe gasped and the shine in her eyes flickered slightly. "Liam? Really?"

Alexis nodded. She was about to read the P.S. when Shiva-Rose asked softly, "Were you hoping they were from Graham?"

"No, not at all!" Chloe's answer came much too quickly to sound true. She smiled, a little shakily. "Liam's my boyfriend, and he really is the sweetest guy. I mean, he's planning to come back." She reached out to indicate the bouquets.

"And he sent me a dozen dozen . . . ouch!"

"You okay?"

"I pricked my finger on a thorn," she said. "I'm bleeding."

"I have Band-Aids in my room," said Shiva-Rose.

With her wounded finger pressed to her lips, Chloe followed Shiva-Rose out of the common room.

Alexis looked at Lindsay, who was looking at the roses.

"There's a P.S." Alexis said.

"Let me guess," said Lindsay. "It says, 'I'm not giving up.'"

"Yep. That's exactly what it says, word for word." She tossed the card on the coffee table. "What was that you were saying about not liking to share?"

Lindsay sighed. She hadn't needed to hear what was written in the P.S. to know that Liam hadn't sent this ridiculous amount of roses to Chloe.

These roses were for her, for Lindsay. And she knew it.

Because all one hundred and forty-four of them were pink.

To Be Continued . . .

Read on for a teaser from Skin Deep,
the next juicy read in the
America's Next Top Model™ series!

"Shiva-Rose!"

Shiva-Rose, who was lying on the floor of the bedroom pounding out a serious circuit of ab crunches, pulled one iPod ear-bud out of her ear. She looked up to see Alexis standing over her, eating a giant soft pretzel.

"Oh . . . hey!" she gasped, pressing pause on the Pussycat Dolls song.

Alexis grinned. "You were, like, totally in the zone, girl!"

"Yeah, and I'm feeling the burn!" Shiva-Rose smiled at her roommate. "What's up?"

"Now that Faye's gone, there are, like, no decent munchies in this whole building, so I went out and got this." Alexis bit into the salty pretzel, then held out a slim white envelope. "When I came back, I happened to check the mail and found *this*. It's for you." She laughed. "Snail mail. I seriously didn't think people communicated like this anymore."

"Neither did I," said Shiva-Rose, taking the envelope. When she saw the handwriting, the postmark stamp, and the return address, she let out a tiny gasp. Suddenly, her fingers seemed to grip the envelope a little more tightly.

Alexis looked concerned. "I hope it's good news," she said.

"Uh . . . I'm sure it is." Shiva-Rose forced herself to look up from the familiar handwriting and smile at Alexis.

Of course, it all depends on how you define 'good.'

Alexis went to the mirror. "Well, I guess if it were a real emergency, whoever it's from would have called or texted, right?"

"Right."

"So . . . no worries."

Alexis frowned at her pretzel. "Except I should probably have some worries about the nine billion carbs in this stupid thing!" She laughed, dropped the remaining half of the pretzel into the wastebasket, and went to the closet. "I think I'm gonna go find a Pilates class and punish myself for eating food off a cart."

"Sounds good," said Shiva-Rose.

"Wanna come?"

"Um, actually, I'm ready for a cool down so I think I'm just gonna go for a walk."

Alexis shrugged. "Cool.

Shiva-Rose hurriedly twisted her dark hair into

a bun on top of her head. She changed out of her sweat shorts into jeans, pulled a thin green hoodie over her tank top, and slipped on her flip-flops. Then she grabbed up her messenger bag and hurried toward the door, tucking the letter into an outside pocket.

She would read it when she got to where she was going.

Wherever that was.

As Shiva-Rose walked, she struggled to focus on the sights and sounds of a midsummer's day in New York City. She knew how lucky she was to be here; so few of her friends at home would ever have such an opportunity.

Shiva-Rose had finally perfected the NYC gait, that no-nonsense power stride that got New Yorkers where they were going quickly and efficiently. On this Saturday in July SoHo was loud, inviting, chaotic, elegant and just plain awesome all at once. Heat radiated from the sidewalk. Bus fumes mingled with the food aromas from Italian, Indian, French, and Thai restaurants. People buzzed around her, toting shiny bags from shops, girls clicking along in their high heels. There were things to buy, things to learn, things to step over carefully (what ever happened to "curb your dog?"), things to taste, and things to remember and to wonder about for the rest of your life. That was New York City! And Shiva-Rose was right here in the middle of it.

Right here in the middle of it thinking about the letter in her bag.

The letter from Rahm.

Handwritten, folded neatly into an envelope, addressed, stamped . . .

Why had he sent a letter?

An e-mail would have been easier, faster.

But nowhere near as sweet.

As Shiva-Rose crossed Houston Street with the crowd, she felt her heartbeat increase.

Seeing Rahm's handwriting on the envelope had had a surprising effect on her; it had given her a feeling like fingertips brushing the back of her neck, or like hearing a whisper in her ear, all the way from Israel. She hadn't needed to see his name, only the bold, confident script in which he'd addressed the envelope. They'd studied together enough times for her to recognize it instantly, the angular penmanship that was somehow boyish and businesslike at the same time. Once, in seventh grade, when they were reviewing a science lesson, she'd noticed her name doodled in the margin of his notebook. He'd said he'd only written it there to remind himself to call her about the homework. She'd believed him.

Shiva-Rose smiled at the memory, and her hand went to where the letter was safely tucked into the outside pocket of her bag. Would it be flawless, the result of several early drafts (so Rahm-like), revised and corrected? Or had he just written it all out in one sitting, letting the words come in a rush, getting his feelings down on paper to send to her halfway around the world? She knew that no matter what the letter said, once she'd read it—and she'd read it more than one time, certainly—she would gently fold it back into its hand-addressed envelope and save it forever.

And that's something you can't quite do with a text message.

Shiva-Rose sighed.

Now all she had to do now was keep walking until she could muster up the guts to read the letter.

Good thing it was a big city.